Perhaps he  interview here

He'd opened his mouth to do just that when she opened her eyes, gave a little wriggle in the chair, and—*wham!*

An image zig-zagged across his brain—a picture of Imogen Lorrimer, standing up to wriggle her way right out of that navy skirt, shrug off the jacket and slowly unbutton the pearl buttons of her white shirt. Before shaking that dark hair free so it tumbled to her shoulders, then sitting back down on that damn red chair and crossing her legs.

A hoarse noise rasped from his throat. What the hell…? *Why?* Where on earth had *that* come from?

It was time to get a grip on this interview—*and* the conversation. A sigh escaped her and for a second his gaze focused on her lips. Hell, this was *not* good. 'Never Mix Business and Pleasure' was a non-negotiable rule.

Dear Reader

I *so* enjoyed writing this book—hey, Montmartre, Paris, and a yurt in the Algarve…what's not to enjoy?

But most of all I loved writing about Imo and Joe—they became totally real to me even while they drove me nuts as they fought the idea of love all the way.

Imo wanted to play it safe and Joe wanted to play by the rules. So when the sparks began to fly in the bedroom *and* out they—and I—were thrown in at the deep end.

I hope you enjoy seeing what they did about it!

Nina xx

BREAKING
THE BOSS'S RULES

BY
NINA MILNE

Published in Great Britain 2014
by Mills & Boon, an imprint of Harlequin (UK) Limited,
Eton House, 18-24 Paradise Road, Richmond, Surrey, TW9 1SR

© 2014 Nina Milne

ISBN: 978-0-263-91162-6

Printed and bound in Spain
by Blackprint CPI, Barcelona

Nina Milne has always dreamt of writing for Mills & Boon®—ever since as a child she discovered stacks of Mills & Boon® books 'hidden' in the airing cupboard. She graduated from playing libraries to reading the books, and has now realised her dream of writing them.

Along the way she found a happy-ever-after of her own, accumulating a superhero of a husband, three gorgeous children, a cat with character and a real library...well, lots of bookshelves.

Before achieving her dream of working from home creating happy-ever-afters whilst studiously avoiding any form of actual housework, Nina put in time as both an accountant and a recruitment consultant. She figures the lack of romance in her previous jobs is now balancing out.

After a childhood spent in Peterlee (UK), Rye (USA), Winchester (UK) and Paris (France), Nina now lives in Brighton (UK), and has vowed never to move again!! Unless, of course, she runs out of bookshelves. Though there is always the airing cupboard...

Other Modern Tempted™ titles by Nina Milne:

HOW TO BAG A BILLIONAIRE

**This and other titles by Nina Milne
are also available in eBook format
from www.millsandboon.co.uk**

For my parents, for believing in me.

PROLOGUE

Dear Diary
My name is Imogen Lorrimer and my life is in a less than stellar place right now.

For a start there is every possibility that my temporary new boss is about to fire me. His name is Joe McIntyre and, just to really mess with my head, he has taken to appearing in my dreams.

Naked.

Last night was particularly erotic. I won't go into detail, but we were in his office and let's just say various positions were involved...as were varying bits of office furniture...glass-topped desk, red swivel chair...

Obviously I know this is thoroughly unprofessional and utterly inappropriate.

In my defence he is gorgeous.

Think sexy rumpled hair—dark brown, a tiny bit long, with a few bits that stick up. Think chocolate—the expensive kind—brown eyes. Think a strong but not too dominant nose. A long face, with a sculpted jaw and clearly defined chin. Oh, and a body to die for—Joe McIntyre is a long, lean fighting machine.

Problem is, however much I appreciate the man in my dreams, the real live clothed version of Joe McIntyre is a ruthless corporate killing machine. He is a troubleshooter who has been called in to overhaul Langley Interior Design and we are all in danger of losing our jobs.

In fact there is every chance he will fire me on the spot tomorrow—especially given my recent screw-up.

I cannot let that happen. I cannot afford to lose my job. Not on top of everything else.

To be specific I am:

Homeless—my scumbag boyfriend, Steve, of three years has just dumped me for his ex—Simone—and thrown me out of the flat we shared. So I am currently living with my BFF—and, whilst I love Mel like the sister I never had, I can only sleep on her pull-out bed for so long. I think I'm cramping her style.

Heartbroken—Steve ticked all the boxes on my 'What I am looking for in a Man' list. I thought he was The One.

Broke—I blew my savings on a romantic holiday for Steve and me. And, unbelievable though this may sound, he is now taking Simone. How humiliating is that?

It's no wonder that I am fantasising in my dreams. My real life sucks.

Time for some ice cream, methinks!

Imogen x

CHAPTER ONE

JOE MCINTYRE LEANT back in the state-of-the-art office chair and picked up the CV from the glass-topped desk.

Imogen Lorrimer. Peter Langley's PA for the past five years.

She of the raven-black hair and wide grey-blue eyes.

Faint irritation twanged Joe's nerves; her looks were irrelevant. 'No Mixing Business and Pleasure'. That was an absolute rule. Along with 'One Night Only' and 'Never Look Back'. From *The Joe McIntyre Book of Relationships*. Short, sweet and easy to use.

Joe gusted out a sigh as his eyes zoned back to his emails. Leila again. Shame the manual didn't tell him how to deal with a blast-from-the-past ex-girlfriend from a time he'd rather forget. But this was not the time to open *that* can of worms—his guilt was still bad enough that he had agreed to attend her wedding, but there was no need to think further about it. Right now he needed to think about this interview.

Imogen Lorrimer had snagged the edge of his vision the moment she'd entered the boardroom two days before, when he'd called an initial meeting of all Langley staff. He'd nodded impatiently at her to be seated and been further arrested by the tint of her eye colour as she'd perched on her chair and aimed a fleeting glance at him from under the straight line of her black fringe. For a fraction of a second he'd faltered in his speech, stopped in his tracks by eyes of a shade that was neither blue nor grey but some-where in between.

Since then he'd stared at her more than once as she scuttled past him in the corridor, dark head down, clearly reluctant to initiate visual contact.

But he was used to people being nervous around him. After all he was a troubleshooter; people knew he had the power to fire them. A power he used where necessary—had in fact already used that morning. So if firing Imogen Lorrimer would benefit Langley Interior Designs he wouldn't hesitate. However attractive he found her.

As if on cue there was a knock at the open office door and Joe looked up.

Further annoyance nipped his chest at the realisation that he had braced himself as if for impact. Imogen Lorrimer was nothing more than an employee he needed to evaluate. There was no need for this disconcerting aware-ness of her.

For a second she hesitated in the doorway, and despite himself his pulse-rate kicked up a notch.

Ridiculous. In her severely cut navy suit, with her dark hair pulled back into a sleek bun, she looked the epitome of professionalism. The least he could do was pretend to be the same. Which meant he had to *stop* checking her out.

'Come in.' He rose to his feet and she walked stiffly across the floor, exuding nervous tension.

'Mr McIntyre,' she said, her voice high and breathy.

'Joe's fine.' Sitting down, he nodded at the chair oppo-site him. 'Have a seat.'

Surely a simple enough instruction. But apparently not. Astonishment rose his brows as Imogen twitched, stared at the red swivel chair for a few seconds, glanced at him, and then back at the chair. Her strangled gargle turned into an unconvincing cough.

Joe rubbed the back of his neck and studied the apparently hypnotic object. As might be expected in an interior designer's office, it was impressive. Red leather, stylish design, functional, comfortable, eye-catching.

But still just a chair.

Yet Imogen continued to regard it, her cheeks now the same shade as the leather.

Impatience caused him to drum his fingers on the desk and the sound seemed to rally her. Swivelling on her sensible navy blue pumps, she stared down at the glass desktop, closed her eyes as though in pain, and then hauled in an audible breath.

'Is there a problem?' he asked. 'Something wrong with the chair?'

'Of course not. I'm sorry,' she said as she lowered herself downwards onto the edge of the chair and clasped her hands onto her lap.

'If it's not the chair then it must be me,' he said. 'I get that you may be a bit nervous. But don't worry. I don't bite.'

Stricken blue eyes met his as she gripped the arms of the chair as though it were a rollercoaster. 'Good to know,' she said. 'Sorry. Um…I'm not usually this nervous. It's just…obviously…well…' Pressing her glossy lips together tightly, she closed her eyes.

Exasperation surged through him. This was the woman Peter Langley had described as 'a mainstay of the company'. It was no bloody wonder Langley was in trouble. Perhaps he should end this interview here and now.

He'd opened his mouth to do just that when she opened her eyes, gave a little wriggle in the chair, and—*wham!*

An image zigzagged across his brain—a picture of Imogen Lorrimer, standing up to wriggle her way right out of that navy skirt, shrug off the jacket and slowly unbutton the pearl buttons of her white shirt. Before shaking that dark hair free so it tumbled to her shoulders, then sitting back down on that damn red chair and crossing her legs.

A hoarse noise rasped from his throat. What the hell…? *Why?* Where on earth had *that* come from?

It was time to get a grip of this interview—*and* the conversation. A sigh escaped her and for a second his gaze focused on her lips. Hell, this was *not* good. 'Never Mix Business and Pleasure' was a non-negotiable rule. His work ethic was sacrosanct—the thought of jeopardising his reputation and ruining his business the way his father had done was enough to bring him out in hives.

So this awareness had to be nixed—no matter how inexplicably tempting Imogen Lorrimer was. His libido needed an ice bath or a night of fun. Preferably the latter—a nice, relaxed, laid-back evening with a woman unconnected to any client. Someone who could provide a no-strings-attached night of pleasure.

In the meantime he needed to concentrate on the matter in hand.

What had Imogen said last? Before she'd frozen into perpetual silence.

'It's just…obviously…what?' he growled.

Imogen caught her bottom lip in her teeth and bit down hard; with any luck the pain would recall her common sense. If it were logistically possible to boot herself around the room she would, and her fingers tingled with the urge to slap herself upside the head.

Enough.

She had had enough of herself.

It was imperative that she keep her job. For herself, but also because if she were here she could do everything in her power to make sure this man didn't shut Langley down.

Peter and Harry Langley had been more than good to her—the least she could do was try to ensure this corporate killing machine didn't chew up their company and spit it out.

Instead of sitting here squirming in embarrassed silence over last night's encounter with a fantasy Joe McIntyre.

Time to channel New Imogen, who fantasised over gazillions of hot men and didn't bat an eyelid.

She moistened her lips and attempted a smile.

Brown eyes locked with hers and for a heartbeat something flickered in their depths. A spark, an awareness—a look that made her skin sizzle. The sort of look that Dream Joe excelled in.

Then it was gone. Doused almost instantly and replaced by definitive annoyance, amplified by a scowl that etched his forehead with the sort of formidable frown that Real Joe no doubt held a first-class degree in.

Straightening her shoulders, she forced herself to meet his exasperated gaze. 'I apologise, Joe. The past few weeks have been difficult and the result was an attack of nerves. I'm fine now, and I'd appreciate it if we could start again.'

'Let's do that.' His words were emphatic as he gestured to her CV. 'You've been Peter's PA for five years—ever since you came out of college. He speaks very highly of you, so why so nervous?'

OK. Here goes.

There was no hiding the fact that she'd screwed up and, given that Joe had been on the premises for two days, there was little doubt he already knew about it. So it was bite the proverbial bullet time.

'I'm sure you've heard about the Anderson project?'

'Yes, I have.'

Stick to the facts, Imogen.

'Then you know I made a pretty monumental mistake.' Her stomach clenched as she relived the sheer horror. 'I ordered the wrong fabric. Yards and yards of it. I didn't realise I'd done that. The team went ahead and used it and the client ended up with truly hideous mustard-coloured curtains and coverings throughout his mansion instead of the royal gold theme we had promised him.'

A shudder racked her body as she adhered her feet in the thick carpet to prevent herself from swivelling in a twist of sheer discomfort on the chair. 'Mistake' was not supposed to be in the Imogen Lorrimer dictionary. To err was inexcusable; her mother had drummed that into her over and over.

'It was awful. Even worse than…' She pressed her lips together.

His eyes flickered to rest on her mouth and a spark ignited in the pit of her tummy.

'Even worse than what?' he demanded.

Nice one, Imogen. Now no doubt Joe was imagining a string of ditzy disasters in her wake.

Tendrils of hair wisped around her face as she shook her head, sacrificing the perfection of her bun for the sake of vehemence. 'It doesn't matter. Honestly. It's nothing to do with work. Just a childhood memory.'

Joe raised his dark eyebrows, positively radiating scepticism. 'You're telling me that you have a childhood disaster that competes with a professional debacle like that?'

He didn't believe her.

'Yes,' she said biting back her groan at the realisation she would have to tell him. She couldn't risk him assuming she was a total mess-up. 'I was ten and I came home with the worst possible report you could imagine.'

Imogen could still feel the smooth edges of the booklet in her hand; her tummy rolled in remembered fear and sadness. *Keep it light, Imogen.*

'Having lied through my teeth all term that I'd been doing brilliantly, I'd pretty much convinced myself I was a genius—so I was almost as upset to discover I wasn't as my mum was.'

The look of raw disappointment on Eva Lorrimer's face

was one that she would never forget, never get used to, no matter how many times she saw it.

'Anyway...' Imogen brushed the side of her temple in an attempt to sweep away the memory. 'I had the exact same hollow, sinking, leaden feeling when I saw the mustard debacle.'

Joe's brown eyes rested on her face with an indecipherable expression; he was probably thinking she was some sort of fruit loop.

'But the point about the Andersen project is that it was a one-off. I have never made a mistake like that before and I can assure you that I never will again.'

Whilst she had no intention of excusing herself, seeing as the word 'excuse' also failed to feature in her vocabulary, she had messed up the day after Steve had literally thrown her onto the street so his ex-girlfriend could move back in. She'd reeled into work, still swaying in disbelief and humiliation. Not that she had any intention of sharing *that* with Joe; she doubted it would make any difference if she did. She suspected Joe didn't hold much truck with personal issues affecting work.

Panic churned in her stomach. The Langleys wouldn't want Joe to fire her. But Peter was in the midst of a breakdown and Harry was stable but still in Intensive Care after his heart attack; neither of them was in a position to worry about *her*.

Leaning forward, she gripped the edge of the desk. 'I'm good at my job,' she said quietly. 'And I'll do anything I can to help keep this company going until Peter and Harry are back.'

Including fighting this man every step of the way if he tried to tear apart what the Langley brothers had built up.

For a second his gaze dropped, and his frown deepened before he gave a curt nod.

'I'll bear it in mind,' he said. 'Now, let's move on. According to Peter this is a list of current projects and obligations.' He pushed a piece of typewritten paper across the desk. 'He doesn't seem very sure it's complete and he referred me to you.'

Imogen looked down at the list and tried to focus on the words and not on Joe's hand. On his strong, capable fingers, the light smattering of hair, the sturdy wrists that for some reason she wanted so desperately to touch. Those hands that in her dreams had wrought such incredible magic.

Grinding her molars, she tugged the paper towards her. 'I'll check this against my organiser.' She bent at the waist to pick up her briefcase. And frowned. Had that strange choking noise been Joe? As she sat up she glanced at him and clocked a slash of colour on his cheekbones.

Focus.

Imogen looked at the paper and then back at her organiser. 'The only thing not on here is the annual Interior Design awards ceremony. It's being held this Wednesday. Peter and Graham Forrester were meant to attend.' She frowned. 'Could be Peter forgot. Or he's changed his mind because the client can't make it. Or he's too embarrassed to face everyone.'

Joe's forehead had creased in a frown and his fingers beat a tattoo on the desk—and there she was, staring at those fingers *again*.

'Tell me more about it.'

'It's a pretty prestigious event. We won in the luxury category for the interior of an apartment we did for Richard Harvey the IT billionaire. He commissioned us to create a love nest for his seventh wife.'

Joe's brows hiked towards his hairline as he whistled. '*Seven?* The man must be a glutton for punishment.'

'He's a romantic,' Imogen said. 'You've got to admire that kind of persistence.'

'No.'

'No, what?'

'No, I *don't* have to admire it. It's delusional. Sometimes dreams have to be abandoned because they aren't possible.'

Easy for him to say—it was impossible to imagine a lean, mean corporate machine having *any* dreams.

'Some dreams,' she agreed. 'But not all. I truly believe that if you persevere and try and you're willing to compromise there is a person out there for everyone.'

After all, she had no intention of giving up finding a man to match her tick list just because she and Steve had gone pear-shaped.

'Richard has just had to try harder than most. And,' she added, seeing the derisory quirk to his lips, 'he and Crystal are very happy—in fact they are in Paris, celebrating their meetiversary.'

'Excuse me?'

'The day they met a year ago. Richard has whisked her off to Paris for a romantic getaway. That's why they can't attend the awards. I hope Richard and Crystal get to celebrate *decades* of meetiversaries.'

'Good for you. *I* hope to show Richard that we value the award we won for decorating his apartment. So, tell me more about the project. Who worked on it?'

'Peter, Graham and me. Peter often lets me get involved with the design side of things as well as the admin stuff.'

Joe's brown eyes assessed her expression and his fingers continued to drum on the desk-top. 'How involved were you on the project?

'I designed both bathrooms.'

'Could you show me?'

'Sure.'

Trepidation twisted her nerves even as she tried to sound calm. Maybe Joe would use this to make his final decision on her job. Or was it something else? There was something unnerving about his gaze; she could almost hear the whir and tick of his brain.

'I'll get the folder.'

Once she'd pulled the relevant portfolio from the filing cabinet at the back of the room she walked back to the desk.

Placing the folder carefully on the glass top, she leaned over to tug the elastic at the corner. *Whoosh*—an unwary breath and she had inhaled a lungful of Joe: sandalwood, and something that made her want to nuzzle into his neck.

No can do. Newsflash, Imogen: this is not a dream—it's for real.

She needed to breathe shallowly and focus—*not* on the way an errant curl of brown hair had squiggled onto the nape of his neck but on demonstrating her design talent.

'The spec was to create something unique to make Crystal feel special.'

'Tough gig.'

'I enjoyed it.'

Back then she'd been living in Cloud Cuckoo Land, absolutely sure that Steve was about to propose to her, and throwing herself into the spirit of the project had been easy. She had enjoyed liaising with Richard over the plan and ideas—loved the fact that the flat was to be a wedding surprise for his wife.

'These are the bathrooms.'

She pointed to the sketches and watched as he flipped through the pages.

'These are good,' he said.

His words vibrated with sincerity and she felt her lips curve up in a smile, his approval warming her chest.

'Thank you. The hammock bath is fab—big enough for two and perfect for the wet room.'

Imogen and Joe, lying naked in the bath… Just keep talking.

'I went for something more opulent for the second bath-room. All fluted pillars and marble. With a wooden hot tub, complete with a table in the middle for champagne.'

Her breath caught in her throat. *Imogen and Joe, play-ing naked footsie... Move on, move on.*

'And this was my *pièce de résistance*. I managed to source sheets threaded with twenty-two-carat gold for the bedroom.'

Oh, hell. Time to stop talking.

Closing the folder, she moved around the desk, willing her feet not to scurry back to the dratted chair.

'Anyway, Graham can take you through the rest of the project.'

'Not possible.'

'Why not?' Imogen studied Joe's bland expression and the penny clanged from on high. 'Have you *sacked* Gra-ham?'

Joe shrugged. 'Graham no longer works for Langley.'

'But...you can't do that.' Outrage smacked her mouth open and self-disgust ran her veins. How could she possi-bly fantasise over a man who could be so callous?

He raised his eyebrows. 'I think you'll find I can.'

'Graham Forrester is one of the best interior design-ers in London. He's Peter's protégé. Why would you get rid of him?'

'That is not your concern.'

Her hands clenched into fists of self-annoyance. She'd let herself relax, been *pleased* that he had approved of her work. Taken her eye off the fact that he had the power to take Langley apart.

'Graham is my friend and my colleague. I went to his wedding last month. He *needs* this job. So of course it's my concern. And it's not only me who will say that. *Everyone* will be concerned. We're like a family here.'

'And that's a good thing, is it?' His tone was dry, yet the words held amusement.

Anger burned behind her ribs. 'Yes, it is.' A wave of her hand in the air emphasised her point. 'We're the interior design version of *The Waltons*. And sacking Graham is the equivalent of killing off John-Boy.'

His lips quirked upwards for a second and frustration stoked the flames of her ire. He could at least take her seriously.

'You *have* to reconsider.'

The smirk vanished as his lips thinned into a line. 'Not happening, Imogen.'

'Then I'll…'

'Then you'll what?' he asked. 'I think you may need to consider whether your loyalty lies with Graham Forrester or with Langley.'

'Is that a threat?'

'It's friendly advice.' Rubbing the back of his neck, he surveyed her for a moment. 'Peter described you as an important part of the company—if you walk out to support Graham, or undermine my position so I'm forced to let you go, the company will lose out.'

Dammit, she couldn't let Peter and Harry down—however much she wanted to tell him to shove his job up his backside. If she were still here maybe she could do something to prevent further disaster…though Lord knew what. Plus, on a practical note, she couldn't add unemployment to her list of woes.

'I'll stay. But for the record I totally disagree with you letting Graham go.'

'Your concerns are noted. Now, I need you to reinstate Langley's presence at the awards ceremony. We're going.'

'What?' Imogen stared at him. '*You* can't possibly mean to go.'

'Why not?'

'Because it will look odd for Graham not to be there. And you being there is hardly going to send out a good message; it's advertising that Langley is in trouble.'

He shook his head. 'It's *acknowledging* that Langley is in trouble and showing we're doing something about it. The head in the sand approach doesn't work.'

The words stung; she knew damn well from personal experience that the head in the sand approach didn't work. 'My head is quite firmly above ground, thank you.'

'Good. Then listen carefully. Whether you believe it or not, I am good at my job. Me being at these awards will re-assure everyone that Langley is back on its feet and ready to roll.' He leant back and smiled a smile utterly devoid of mirth. 'So we're going. You and me.'

Say what? Imogen stared at him, her chin aiming for her knees.

Joe nodded. 'You worked on the project, you liaised with the client—it makes sense.'

CHAPTER TWO

IMOGEN PACED HER best friend's lounge, striding over the brightly flowered rug, past the camp bed she was currently spending her nights on, to the big bay-fronted window and back again. 'Makes sense!' She narrowed her eyes at Mel and snorted. 'Makes sense, my…'

Mel shifted backwards on the overstuffed sofa, curled her legs under her and rummaged in her make-up bag. 'Imo, hun… You need to calm down. Joe is in charge and you have no choice.' Holding up two lipsticks, she tilted her blonde head to one side in consideration. 'It may even be fun.'

'Fun?' Imogen stared at her, a flicker of guilt igniting as her tummy did a loop-the-loop of anticipation. 'Fun to spend two hours working late with Joe and then going to an awards ceremony with Joe. That's not fun. It's purgatory.'

Mel raised her perfectly plucked eyebrows. 'Imo! Imo! Imo! Methinks you protest too much. Methinks you fancy the boxers off the man.'

There was that fire of guilt again. How could she be so shallow as to have the hots for such an arrogant, ruthless bastard?

'Youthinks wrong,' Imogen said flatly. 'And why are you looking at me like that?'

'A) Because you couldn't lie your way out of a paper bag and B) because I'm hoping you aren't planning to go to the awards ceremony looking like that.'

Imogen looked down at herself. 'What's wrong with

this? I wore this to a big client dinner with Steve a few months ago.'

'Exactly.'

'What is that supposed to mean?'

'Imogen, sweetie. That dress is *dull*. It's grey and it's shapeless and it's boring. It's how Steve liked you to dress because he was terrified you would run off—like Simone did.'

'That's not true. I chose this dress because…' She trailed off. 'Anyway, it will have to do. In fact with any luck no one will notice me. I mean, it's wrong to go to the awards ceremony when Graham did most of the work.'

Mel frowned. 'It sounds to me like you did your fair share. Plus, Graham can't go because he doesn't work for Langley any more. Plus, you said that Joe said he would still be credited.'

'Humph…' Damn man had an answer to everything.

'So you are going to this ceremony to display to the world that Langley is alive and flourishing. If you go dressed like that everyone will think Langley is on its last legs and you've bought a dress for the funeral.'

'Ha-ha!' Imogen exhaled a sigh as she contemplated her best friend's words. Mel knew all there was to know about clothes, and she had a point. 'OK. How about my little black dress with…?'

'It's more big black bin-bag, Imo. I have a way better idea. You can borrow one of *my* dresses.'

'Um…Mel. You know me. I really, really don't want to be…'

'The focus of attention? Yes, you do. And I've got the perfect outfit. Wait here a second.'

Imogen exhaled a puff of air—of course she wanted to do the right thing for Langley, but she knew Mel, and her friend's fashion taste was nothing like hers. Imogen's taste was more…

More what? In a moment of horror she realised she didn't know. In all her twenty-six years she'd always dressed to please others.

Eva Lorrimer had had very firm ideas about what a young girl should wear, and at her insistence Imogen had obediently donned plain long skirts and frilly tops. It had seemed the least she could do to make her mum a little bit happy. Plus, anything for a quiet life—right?

Then Steve… Well, was Mel right? *Had* she let him dictate what she wore? Steve had always said he hated women who flaunted or flirted when they were in a relationship. He had told her how Simone had always done exactly that. So she'd worked out what he approved of and what he liked and taken care to shop accordingly. Because it had made her happy to make him happy. Plus, anything for a quiet life—right?

Mel waltzed back into the room. 'What do you think?'

Imogen stared at the dress Mel was holding up. If you could even call it a dress. For the life of her she couldn't work out how she would get into it, or where all the lacy frou-frou would go, or even how it could even be decent. The only thing that was clear was the colour—bright, vibrant and sassy.

'It's very…red.'

OK. It wasn't what *she* would choose. But if she had the choice between something in her wardrobe chosen by her mum or Steve and something chosen by Mel, right now she was going with Mel's choice.

'I'll wear it.'

Mel blinked. 'Really? I was prepared for battle.'

'Nope. No battle. Though you may have to help me work out how to put it on.'

'I'll do better than that—I'll lend you shoes and do your make-up as well.'

'Perfect. Thanks, sweetie. You're a star.'

Surprise mixed with a froth of anticipation as to what this New Imogen would look like.

An hour later and she knew.

Staring at the image that looked back at her from the mirror, she blinked, disbelief nearly making her rub her eyes before taking another gander. Her mother would keel over in a faint, Steve's lips would purse in disapproval—and Imogen didn't care. She looked....*visible*.

'You look gorgeous. You look hot. Joe McIntyre won't know what's hit him.'

'I'm not doing this for Joe.'

Liar, liar, pants most definitely on fire.

Squashing the voice, she gave her head a small shake. The butterflies currently completing an assault course in her tummy were nothing to do with Joe.

'I'm doing it for Langley.'

Mel dimpled at her. 'You keep telling yourself that, Imo,' she said soothingly. 'Have fun!'

Joe glanced around the office and gusted out a sigh. Not that there was anything to complain about in the surroundings; he'd sat in far worse than this mecca to interior design and it hadn't bothered him. The problem was that wherever he was sitting he'd never had this level of anticipation twisting his gut.

Irritation stamped on his chest. Anticipation had no place here. The awards ceremony would go better for Langley if Imogen Lorrimer were there. She had worked on the Richard Harvey project, knew many of the people who would be there, so it made sense for her to attend.

Joe snorted and picked up his cup of coffee. Listen to himself. Anyone would think he was justifying his decision because he had an ulterior motive in taking Imogen. When of course he didn't. Or that he was looking forward to taking Imogen. Which was ridiculous. The woman couldn't stand him, and he had the definitive suspicion that she was planning some sort of rearguard action against him in the hope that he'd change his mind about Graham Forrester.

She was probably running a Bring Back John-Boy Campaign.

Yet in the past two days he had more than once, more than twice, more than…too many times…found himself looking for Imogen or noticing her when there'd been no need to. Caught by the turn of her head or a waft of her delicate flowery perfume.

Exasperation surfaced again and he quelled it. Just because her appearance had somehow got under his guard it didn't mean there was a problem. He knew all too well the associated perils of letting personal issues into the boardroom. That was what his father had done and the result had been a spiral of disaster—a mess bequeathed to Joe to sort out.

So there was no problem. All he had to do was recall the grim horror of working out that his family firm was bankrupt and corrupt. Remember the faces of the people he'd been forced to let go, the clients whose money had been embezzled.

Enough. The lesson was learnt.

His computer pinged to indicate the arrival of an email; one glance at the screen and he groaned. *Another* email from Leila. Every instinct jumped up and down—he was no expert on the intricacies of relationships, but he was pretty damn sure it wasn't normal for an ex to suddenly surface after seven years, invite him to her wedding and then email him regularly to give him advice he hadn't asked for.

Resisting the urge to thump his head on the desk, he looked up as the door rebounded off its hinges and Imogen entered.

No. She didn't enter. It was more of a storm… A vivid

red tornado of gorgeous anger headed straight towards him and slammed her palms down on the glass desk-top.

'Something wrong?' Joe asked, trying and failing to ignore the sleek curtain of hair that fell straight and true round her face and down past her shoulders to the plunging V of her dress. Surely there was more V than material?

Continuing his look downward, he took in the cinched-in waist and the flouncy skirt that hit a good few centimetres above the knee. Her legs were endless, long and toned, and ended in a pair of sparkly peep-toe sandals.

Stop looking. Before you have a coronary.

He tugged his gaze upward to meet a fulminating pair of grey-blue eyes.

'Yes, there *is* something wrong.'

Her breath came in pants and Joe clenched his jaw, nearly crossing his eyes in an attempt to remain focused on her face.

'I know I shouldn't say anything. I know I shouldn't put my job on the line. But I've just come from seeing Harry and Peter in the hospital and they told me that you've got rid of Maisey in Accounts and Lucas in Admin. How could you? It's *wrong*.'

The fury vibrating in her voice touched a chord in him, aroused an answering anger to accompany the frustration and self-annoyance already brewing in his gut.

'No, Imogen, it isn't wrong. It's *unfortunate*. Streamlining Langley is the only way for the company to survive. I'd rather a few people suffer than the whole company collapse.'

She huffed out air and shook her head, black hair shimmering. 'But don't you care?' she asked. 'It's like these people are just numbers to you.'

The near distaste in her eyes made affront claw down his chest. 'I do my very best to minimise the number of people I let go and I certainly don't take any pleasure in it.'

She stood back from the desk and slammed her hands on her hips. 'You don't seem to feel any pain either.'

Her words made him pause; sudden discomfort jabbed his nerves. It was an unease he dismissed; feeling pain sucked, and it didn't change a damn thing. This he knew. Hell, he had the whole wardrobe to prove it. So if he'd hardened himself it was a *good* thing—a business decision that made him better at his job.

Aware of curiosity dancing with anger across Imogen's delicate features, he shrugged. 'Me sitting around crying into my coffee isn't going to enable me to make sensible executive decisions. I can't let sentiment interfere with my job.'

'But what if your executive choices hurt someone else?'

'I don't make choices to hurt people.'

'That doesn't mean they don't *get* hurt. Look at Graham. I happen to know he has a large mortgage, his wife is pregnant, and now you've made the choice to snatch his job from under his feet. Doesn't that bother you?'

'No.' To his further exasperation he appeared to be speaking through clenched teeth. 'The bottom line is I do the best for the company as whole. Overall, people benefit.'

'Have you ever watched *Star Trek*?'

Star Trek? Joe blinked. 'Yes, I have. My sisters are avid fans.' Repeats of the show had been a godsend in the devastating months after their parents' death; Tammy and Holly had spent hours glued to the screen. Blocking out impossible reality with impossible fiction.

'Joe? Are you listening to me?'

'For now. But only because I am fascinated to see what pointy-eared aliens and transporters have to do with anything?'

'You know how it works—they *say* they believe in sacrificing the few for the many. But they don't really mean it—somehow in real life they end up knowing that it's wrong and they go back to rescue one person, risking everyone, and everything is OK.'

Was she for real? 'The fatal flaw in your reasoning is right there. *Star Trek* isn't real life. It's *fiction*.'

'I get that—but the principle is sound.'

'No. The principle sucks. If you run around trying to please everyone, refusing to make tough choices, then I can tell you exactly what happens. Everyone suffers.' He'd got another wardrobe to prove *that*. 'In real life Kirk would go down, and so would the *Enterprise*.'

'That is so…'

'Realistic?'

'Cynical,' she snapped. 'I don't understand why you can't see reason. The main reason Langley is in difficulties is because of Harry's ill health. He's the one who understands finance. Peter doesn't. Once Harry's on his feet everything will go back to normal. Surely you should be taking that into consideration? Trying to think of some way to salvage everyone's jobs.'

The jut of her chin, the flash of her eyes indicated how serious she was, and although he had no doubt his decisions were correct, it occurred to him that it was a long, long time since anyone had questioned him, let alone locked phasers with him. Apart from his sisters, anyway…

It was kind of…exhilarating.

Even more worrying, his chest had warmed with admiration: Imogen was speaking out for others with a passion that made him think of a completely different type of passion. His fingers itched with the desire to bury themselves in the gloss of her dark hair and angle her face so that he could kiss her into his way of thinking.

For the love of Mike… This was so off the business plan he might as well file for bankruptcy right now.

Curving his fingers firmly round the edge of his desk, he adhered his feet to the plush carpet and forced calm to his vocal cords. 'My job is to make sure that Harry has a viable company to come back to. I am not out to destroy Langley. That's not how I operate.'

'That's not what your reputation says.'

Disbelief clouded her blue eyes with grey and the disdain in her expression caused renewed affront to band round his chest.

'Imogen, there are some companies that even I can't salvage. But if you study my track record you will see that most of the companies I go to sort out get sorted out. Not shut down. My reputation is that I'm tough. I'll make the unpopular decisions no one wants to make because they let sentiment and friendship cloud their perspective. I don't.'

A small frown creased her brow. 'So you're telling me you're cold and heartless but you get results?'

'Yes. Peter and Harry wouldn't be able to let Graham go. I can. They, you and Captain Kirk may not like my methods, but I *will* save Langley.'

Annoyance at the whole conversation hit him—talk about getting overheated. Who did he think he was? The corporate version of the Lone Ranger? He'd spent the better part of the past half an hour justifying his actions, and he was damned if he knew why. Anyone would think he *cared* about her opinion of him.

'Now, can you please sit down so we can get some work done?'

At least that way the bottom half of her would be obscured from sight and his blood pressure would stay on the chart.

Imogen dropped down onto the chair. Joe's words were ringing in her head—and there was no doubting his sincerity. So, whilst she saw him as the villain of the piece he saw himself as the hero.

She chewed her bottom lip—was there any chance that

he was right? Then she remembered Harry Langley's pale face, blending in with the colour of his hospital pillow. His slurred voice shaking with impotent anger as he vowed to put things right.

She thought of the size of Graham's mortgage, his pride that his wife could be a stay-at-home mum if she wanted... of Maisey's tears when she'd phoned her on the way here from the hospital...

All those people suffering because of the man sitting opposite her.

Yet a worm of doubt wriggled into her psyche. His deep voice had been genuine when he'd spoken of the necessity of his cuts, the bigger picture, his desire to save Langley.

But, hell, that didn't mean she had to *like* him. Nonetheless...

'Imogen.'

His impatient growl broke into her reverie.

'Did you hear a word I said?'

'Sorry. I was thinking it must be hard to always be seen as the villain,' she replied.

'Doesn't bother me.' A quizzical curve tilted his lip. 'You starting to feel sorry for me now?'

'Of course not.'

The idea was laughable; Joe McIntyre didn't need sympathy. He needed to be shaken into common sense and out of her dreams.

'Well, tonight we need to at least call a truce. You acting as though I am some sort of corporate monster will do more damage to Langley than I can. So you need to play nice.'

Wrinkling her nose in a way that she could only hope indicated distaste, she nodded. Instinct told her a truce with this man would be dangerous, but he was right: they could hardly attend the award ceremony sparring with each other.

'As long as you know I am playing. As in pretending.'

'Don't worry,' he said, his voice so dry it was practically parched. 'Message received, loud and clear. The truce is temporary. Now, can we get on with it? I've ordered a taxi to take us to the hotel at seven, and I want to go through Peter's client list with you before then.'

An hour later Imogen put her pen down. 'I think that's it,' she said.

Flexing her shoulders, she looked across at him. Big mistake. Because now she couldn't help but let her gaze linger on the breadth of his chest under the snowy-white dress shirt and the tantalising hint of bare skin on show where he hadn't bothered doing up the top buttons.

Looking up, she caught a sudden predatory light in his brown eyes. A light that was extinguished almost before she could be sure it had been there, but yet sent a shiver through her body.

'You've done a great job.' Pulling at the sheaf of paper she'd scribbled on, he glanced down at her notes.

'Thank you. I'll type those up for you first thing tomorrow. The notes indicate what each project was, how many times they've used us, and a few personal bits about them. Not *personal* personal, but...'

Babble-babble-babble. One probably imagined look and she'd dissolved into gibberish.

'Things that show I'm not delivering the same spiel to each client,' he said. 'Exactly what I need.'

He stared down at the paper and cleared his throat, as if searching for something else to say. Could he be feeling the same shimmer of tension she was?

'So...according to this, you've done a lot of actual design work.'

'Er...yes... I told you I help out.'

'I didn't realise how much. Why haven't you put all the project work you've done on your CV? Or, for that matter, why haven't you put things on a more formal footing? I'm sure Peter would agree to sponsor you so you could go to college.'

'That's not the way I want my career to go.'

It was a decision made long ago. What she prized above all else was security—a job she enjoyed, but not one that would rule her life. She'd seen first-hand the disastrous consequences of a job that became an obsession, and she wasn't going there.

'Why not? You've got real talent and great client liaison skills. Everyone I've spoken to so far has only had good things to say about you—even Mike Anderson.' He nodded at the paper. 'From everything you've written there, it seems clear they'll all be the same.'

Imogen couldn't help the smile that curved her lips as she savoured his words, absorbed them into her very being. 'Everyone? Even Mike Anderson? For real?'

'For real.'

He smiled back and, dear Lord above, what a smile it was. Instinct told her it rarely saw the light of day—and what a good thing *that* was for the female population. Because it was the genuine make-your-knees-go-weak article.

The moment stretched, the atmosphere thickening around them, blanketing them...

'So what do you think?' Joe asked.

'About what?' *Focus, Imo.*

'Changing career? Within Langley if it remains a viable option. Or elsewhere.'

Forcing herself to truly concentrate on his question, she let the idea take hold. New Imogen Lorrimer—wearer of red dresses and trainee interior designer. *Yeah, right.* There was no version of Imogen who would leap out of her comfort zone like that.

And she was fine with that. More than fine. The whole point of a comfort zone was that it was *comfortable*.

'Not for me, thank you. I'm very happy as I am.'

End of discussion; there was no need for this absurd urge to justify herself.

Glancing at her watch, she rose to her feet and pushed the chair backwards. 'Look at the time. I need to get ready before the taxi gets here.'

An audible hitch of breath was her only answer, and she looked up from her watch to see dark brown eyes raking over her. Without her permission her body heated up further—a low, warm glow in her tummy to accompany the inexplicable feeling of disappointment at a decision she knew to be right.

'You look pretty ready to me,' he drawled.

Was he flirting with her? Was she dreaming?

An unfamiliar spark, no doubt ignited by the sheer effrontery of the dress, lit up a synapse in her brain. Hooking a lock of hair behind her ear, she fought the urge to flutter her eyelashes.

'Is that a compliment?'

'If you want.'

There was that look again—and this time she surely wasn't imagining the smoulder. Even if she had no idea how to interpret it.

'It's also an observation.'

As he rose to his feet and picked up a black tie from the back of his chair Imogen gulped. Six foot plus of lean, honed muscle.

'So,' he continued, 'seeing as you had a bathroom break a quarter of an hour ago, my guess is that you're avoiding this discussion. True or false?'

Mesmerised, she watched his strong fingers deftly pull the tie round his neck before he turned and picked his jacket up.

'False…' she managed.

Right now she needed to get away from the pheromone onslaught—she *wasn't* avoiding the discussion. Much…

'If you say so.' Slinging the jacket over his shoulder, he headed towards her. 'And, Imogen? One more thing?'

'Yes?'

Oh, hell—he was getting closer. Why weren't her feet moving? Heading towards the door and the waiting taxi? Instead her ridiculous heels appeared superglued to the carpet as her heart pounded in her ribcage. A hint of his earthy scent tickled her nostrils, and still her stupid feet wouldn't obey her brain's commands.

His body was so warm…his eyes held hers in thrall. Hardly able to breathe, she clocked his hand rising, and as he touched her lower lip heat shot through her body.

A shadow fleeted across his face and he stepped backwards, his arm dropping to his side.

'Don't forget to smile,' he said.

CHAPTER THREE

IMOGEN DUCKED INTO a corner of the crowded room, needing a moment to breathe after an hour of smiling, socialising and being visible. The set-up was gorgeous—worthy of the five-star hotel where the event was being held. Glorious flower arrangements abounded, in varying shades of pink to fuchsia, layered with dark green foliage. Chandeliers glinted and black-suited waiters with pink ties appeared as if by magic with trays of canapés or a choice of pink champagne and sparkling grapefruit juice.

Surreptitiously she slipped one foot out of a peep-toe, six-inch heeled shoe. Flexing it with relief, she let her gaze unerringly sift through the crowds of beautiful professionals, slip over the fabulously decorated room, heady with the fragrance of the magnificent spring flower centre-pieces that adorned each table, and found the tall figure of Joe McIntyre.

If it really was Joe and not some sort of clone.

Because ever since they'd walked through the imposing doors of the hotel Joe had undergone some sort of trans-formation. It had been goodbye to her taxi companion, Mr Dark and Brooding, and hello Mr Suave as he networked the room, all professional charm and bonhomie, not a sin-gle frown in sight.

But worst of all had been his closeness, the small touches as he'd propelled her from person to person, dis-pensing confidence in Langley and an insider knowledge of interior design that was impressive.

Little surprise that he had gathered a gang of female groupies who were now hanging on to his every word adoringly.

'What's wrong, Imo? That's a pretty hefty scowl. Contemplating the man who'll bring Langley down?'

Shoving her foot back into her shoe, Imogen turned and plastered her best fake smile to her face. *Great!* The man she'd been avoiding all night: head of IMID, Langley's chief competitor.

'Evening, Ivan. How are you?'

'I'm fine. Bursting with health. Which is more than can be said for poor old Harry and Peter. How *are* they?'

Imogen's skin crawled as Ivan Moreton's grey eyes slid over her with almost reptilian interest. Ivan had no principles or scruples, and had engaged in so many underhand schemes to undercut and undermine Langley that she'd lost count.

His methods were unscrupulous, but legal. So to hear him stand there, full of spuriously concerned queries as to Peter and Harry made her blood sizzle. Especially when he looked as though he could barely stop himself from rubbing his hands together in glee.

'Firmly on the road to recovery, thank you, Ivan. I'll be sure to tell them you were asking as a further incentive to get them back into the office.'

To wipe that smug smirk off your face.

'If, of course, they have an office to return to,' Ivan said, with a wave in Joe's direction. 'Could be that Mr McIntyre will have sold it off.'

'Joe wouldn't do that.' Imogen clamped her lips together; had there been a note of *hero-worship* in her voice? Please, no…

Ivan's eyebrows rose. 'Don't be deceived by those rugged looks, Imo. Joe McIntyre will do what it takes. Though even *he* makes mistakes. You see, Graham Forrester now works for me—and he's one very angry designer. Imagine offering him a salary cut. Graham said he's never been so insulted in his life.'

Imogen blinked as she tried to process that little snippet of information.

True, Graham couldn't afford a salary cut—but Peter had given Graham his first break, shown faith in him, showered him in pay rises. Shouldn't loyalty count for something? At least enough for Graham not to feel insulted and maybe not go straight to Langley's biggest competitor?

Or perhaps everyone else in the world got it except her? Were all capable of making executive decisions without sentiment?

Imogen took a step backwards, uncomfortably aware that whilst she had been thinking Ivan had stepped straight into her personal space. Enough so that now the coolness of the wall touched the bare skin on her back. If he came any closer, so help her, she'd either punch him on the nose or—better yet—take a step forward and pinion him with her heel.

'Joe won't be selling off the offices because there will be no need to,' she stated. 'Langley is still alive and kicking—and hopefully we'll be kicking *your* sorry behind for a long time to come.'

'Dream on, Imo. But I like your style.'

His cigarette-infused breath, tinted with alcohol, hit her cheek and she turned her face away.

'When I buy Langley out I'll put in a special bid for you.'

Ewwww. No one would thank her for creating a scene, but enough was enough. Imogen lifted her foot.

'Sounds like you need to be talking to *me*, Ivan.'

Imogen expelled a sigh of relief as she heard Joe's drawl, and then she looked up and saw the glint of anger in his eyes. She spotted the set jaw and something thrilled in-side her.

Get some perspective, Imo.

For a start she was quite capable of looking after her-self, and had had a perfectly good self-defence plan. Plus, Ivan was planning a Langley buy-out—*that* was what she needed to be thinking about. Instead of going all gooey because Joe was being protective.

The interior designer spun round and held his hand out. 'Joe. My friend. How are you doing? Imogen and I were just—'

'I can see exactly what *you* were just doing, Ivan, and I'd appreciate it if *you* didn't do it again.'

Ivan's grey eyes flicked from Imogen to Joe. 'You call-ing dibs, my friend?'

Imogen gave a small gasp. *Please let it have sounded like outrage, not hope.*

'No.' Joe stepped forward, his lips curling in a smile that held no mirth whatsoever. 'But if you want to talk about Langley deal with me. Not anyone else.'

The interior designer gave a toss of his dyed blond hair and stepped backwards. 'I'll do that. I'll get my PA to call your PA and set something up. I'm *very* interested in a buy-out.'

With that he turned and walked away.

'You OK?'

'I'm fine.' Imogen waved away his look of concern. 'Ivan Moreton is a sleazebag, and if you hadn't turned up he'd have been on his way to A&E with a stiletto through his foot.'

This time Joe's smile was real, and Imogen's stomach rollercoastered, all focus leaving the building.

'It's time for the presentations,' Joe said.

So not the moment to discuss the impossibility of an

IMID buy-out; plus, it would best to do that out of Ivan's range.

'I'll text Richard.'

'Why? What happened to the romantic Parisian get-away?'

'Nothing. He wants to show his support so I've arranged for him to be video conferenced in.'

'Great idea? Yours?'

There was that warmth again at his words... She needed to stop being so damn needy of people's approval. Just because praise had been a rarity in her childhood it didn't mean she had to overreact to it.

'Thanks,' she said, as coolly as she could, and quickly bent over her phone to hide the flush of pleasure that touched her cheeks.

A minute later her phone vibrated and she glanced down at it and blinked. Read the words again and gave a small whoop under her breath.

'Good news?'

'Yup. Look. That's Richard. He and Crystal have bought a place in Paris and they want us to pitch for the job of doing it up.' She continued reading. 'He wants us—you and me—to meet him in Paris on Friday.'

Joe and Imogen off to Paris. Be still her beating heart.

Polite applause broke out around them as the first speaker mounted the podium.

'That's excellent news. You'd better book some tickets on the Eurostar, then.'

Was that all he had to say? Was she the only one all of a flutter here? Of course she was. After all she was the one with the dream problem.

Turning away from him, Imogen stared resolutely at the speaker and tried to focus on his words. For the rest of the evening she would focus on interior design. *Not* on the man sitting beside her.

* * *

'Paris?' A pyjama-clad Mel stared at her in sheer disbelief. 'You are going to *Paris* with Joe McIntyre?'

'Yes.' Imogen snuggled back on the sofa and cradled her mug of hot chocolate. 'Ironic, really. I practically begged Steve to take me there, but he wouldn't. Said it held too many memories of Simone.'

She took a gulp of hot chocolate and pushed away memories of just how much time she had spent choosing a cruise that didn't contain any locations holding any memories of Simone. There was *real* irony for you. Because right this minute now Steve and Simone were on that luxury cruise, paid for with *her* hard-earned money, creating new memories.

'I'd rather go with someone hot like Joe than Steve,' Mel said musingly.

'That's plain shallow,' Imogen said. 'Heat level isn't everything in a man, you know. There are other attributes that are way more important.'

The sort of traits *she* looked for in a partner: kindness, stability, loyalty, security. More irony—how had she misjudged Steve so badly?

Mel shook her head, blonde curls bobbing. 'Not if you're on a jaunt to Paris.'

'It's not a *jaunt*. It's a business trip. We're not even staying overnight. Joe is out of the office tomorrow, I'm meeting him at St Pancras Station on Friday late morning, then we're coming back straight after our meeting.'

'*Tchah!* Why don't you book the wrong tickets by "mistake"? Then you could end up staying in a romantic hotel and…'

'I'd end up fired.'

Though for one stupid, insane moment her imagination had leapt in… She could see the hotel silhouetted on the Parisian horizon…

Imogen drained her mug. 'I'm for bed.'

'Oh!' Mel gave a gasp. 'I was so gobsmacked by Paris I forgot to tell you. Your mum called—she said it was urgent. Not *that* sort of urgent,' she added hastily, seeing panic grip her friend as she imagined the worst. 'But she did say you needed to ring her back, no matter what time it was.'

Imogen sighed. This wasn't what she needed right now, but Eva Lorrimer hated being made to wait.

Grabbing her mobile phone from the floor, she dialled her mother. 'Hey, Mum. It's me.'

'Finally.'

'Sorry. The awards ceremony finished late.'

'I only hope you going means you'll keep your job, Imogen. You make sure you impress Joe McIntyre. *Somehow*. Good PAs are two a penny, and now you've managed to lose Steve you will need to support yourself and—'

'Mum. Mel said it was urgent?' Surely reciting all Imogen's shortcomings couldn't be classed as imperative at past midnight. Even by Eva's standards.

'It *is* urgent. Steve has proposed to Simone on that cruise he's taken her on. They're getting married.'

Breath whooshed out of her lungs; surely this was some sort of joke. 'How do you know?'

'Clarissa rang me with the news.'

Better and better—Imogen bit back a groan. Clarissa was Steve's mother and one of Eva's old schoolfriends. If you could call her a friend. No doubt she had rung up to gloat.

'It's all over social media too,' Eva continued. 'Simone even put out a message thanking you for providing such a wonderful setting.'

Excellent. Now she'd be a laughing stock to everyone who knew her. Humiliation swept over her in a wave of heat that made her skin clammy.

Eva gusted out a sigh. 'That could have been *you* if you'd played your cards right. *You* could have a man to rely on—a man to support you and keep you secure. You should have done more to keep him, Imogen.'

Like what? She'd done everything she could think of to make Steve happy. Obviously she'd failed. Big-time. Steve himself had told her that she wasn't enough for him.

But instead of the usual self-criticism a sudden spark of anger ignited in the pit of her stomach. The bastard had actually proposed to another woman on the cruise *she* had paid for using her hard-earned savings. What would he do next? Send her the bill for the engagement ring?

'Actually, Mum, maybe I'm better off without him.'

'Steve was the best thing that ever happened to you, Imogen. Yes, I'd have preferred a fast-track banking career for you, but the next best thing would have been marrying a man with one...'

As Eva's voice droned on Imogen ground her molars and waited for the right moment to intercede.

'Mum. I understand how you feel.' That her daughter had let her down yet again. 'But I'm exhausted. We'll talk more tomorrow.'

Imogen disconnected the call and resisted the urge to bang her head against the wall.

Joe glanced at his watch, and then around the busy Victorian-style St Pancras station. Men and women tapped onto tablets, sipped at coffee or shopped in the boutiques. But there was no sign of Imogen. Where the hell *was* she?

Ah. There she was: striding across the crowded lounge, briefcase in one hand, cup of coffee in the other, dove-grey trouser suit, hair tugged up into a simple ponytail.

'Sorry I'm late,' she stated as she came to a halt next to him.

Joe frowned; her tone indicated not so much as a hint

of sincerity. In fact it pretty much dared him to comment. Imogen seemed… He glanced at her coffee cup as she tugged the lid off. Full. Yet she seemed wired—there was a pent-up energy in the tapping of her foot, an unnecessary force as she dropped her briefcase onto a chair.

'No problem. We've still got three minutes till we need to board.'

'Good.' She took a gulp of coffee. 'Then I have time to grab a *pain au chocolat*. Get myself in the mood.'

Because what she *really* needed right now was sugar on top of caffeine.

Joe swallowed the words. As a man who had brought up twin sisters, he knew exactly when it was best to keep his opinions to himself.

Clearly something had happened in the day and a half since he'd last seen her. But equally clearly Imogen's private life was nothing to do with him.

So he was *not* going to ask her what was wrong; he was going to stick to business.

Focusing on her back, he followed Imogen through the departure lounge to the ticket barriers, where they were smiled through by a svelte member of Eurostar staff. They moved along the bustling platform and onto the train.

He waited until she'd tucked her briefcase next to her and sat down opposite him, her eyes still snapping out that 'don't mess with me' vibe.

'So, could you brief me on our meeting with Richard Harvey? Has he told you anything about the project at all?'

'Nope. All I know is that it's a place in Paris. He's also said he's giving Graham a chance to pitch for it as well, because it seems only fair.' She frowned. 'My guess is Graham got on the phone and guilted him into it with a sob story about how you had brutally thrown him out.'

Joe raised his eyebrows. 'I thought you agreed with him?'

'I do, but…' Her slim shoulders lifted in a shrug and her

eyes sparked. 'If you must know Graham rang me yesterday, and he was really vindictive. Not only about you but about Peter too—and that's not fair. It's not as though *Peter* sacked him. And even *you* offered him a reduced salary.'

'You told me yourself about his mortgage and his wife; you can't blame him for accepting a more lucrative offer and now being loyal to Ivan.'

'I can blame whoever I like for whatever I like.'

Joe blinked at the sheer vehemence of her tone.

'Anyway,' she went on, 'Ivan is an out-and-out toad.' The description brought a small quirk to his lips until she said, 'And you aren't going to let him buy out Langley, are you?'

Damn. He'd hoped she'd forgotten that, but maybe this was why she was on the warpath.

'That's not something I can discuss with you.'

'But…you can't be seriously thinking about it. It would kill Harry off.'

'If a buy-out is offered I have to consider it.'

She opened her mouth as if to argue but inhaled deeply instead. 'OK. Fine. Clearly you don't have a better nature to appeal to, so tell me what I can do to help avert a buy-out.' Her fingers encircled the plastic table's edge and her nose wrinkled in distaste. 'Because I'd rather starve in a ditch than work for Ivan.'

He could hardly blame her; a sudden wave of aversion washed over him at the very thought. Irritation with himself clenched his jaw. If the buy-out was best for Langley that was the road he'd take. Full stop.

'That will be your choice. My decision will be based on what's best for Langley as a business.'

Eyes narrowed, she tapped a foot on the carriage floor. 'If we win this Paris project will that make Langley safe from Ivan?'

'Depends on the full extent of the project. But, yes, it would help.'

'So you're fully on board with going all out to win it? You haven't already decided that the buy-out is the way to go?'

Joe resisted the urge to roll his eyes. Why didn't she get that the decision was nothing to do with her?

'Can we drop the subject of the buy-out and concentrate on winning the Richard Harvey project? What else can you tell me about Richard and this meeting that will help our pitch? Is he bringing wife number seven?'

'Yes. I've told you her name is Crystal—and obviously don't make a big deal of her being number seven.'

Joe snorted. 'Well, gee, Imogen—thanks for the advice. *My* plan was to ask for a rundown of each and every wife along with a view of the wedding albums.' He gusted out a sigh. 'I'll happily avoid the entire topic of marriage.'

Imogen shook her head. 'Richard likes talking about marriage. Like I said, he's incurably romantic—which I suppose is why he's bought a place in Paris. As far as he is concerned he has finally fulfilled his dream—he's found The One. So probably best *not* to share your "dreams should be abandoned" theory.' Her eyes narrowed. 'Even if I'm beginning to wonder if you're right.'

'Me? Right? Wonders will never cease.' Curiosity won out over common sense. 'What brought that on?'

Opening her mouth as if to answer, her gaze skittered away as she clearly thought better of it and shook her head. 'You know, the daft dreams we have when we are young. I once thought I'd become an artist—had some stupid vision of myself in smock and beret, sketching on the streets of Paris or attending the Royal Academy, studying the masters in Italy, exhibiting in Rome—' She broke off. 'Absurd.'

Yet the look in her eyes, the vibrant depth of her tone, showed him that the dream had been real.

Lord knew he could empathise with giving up a dream. For a second he was transported back to a time when the world had truly been his oyster. He could smell the sea spray, taste the tang of salt in his mouth, feel the thump of exhilaration as he rode a wave. The incredible freedom, the knowledge that he would win the championships, would get sponsored, would...

Would end up dealing with bereavement, loss and responsibility.

Whoa. There was no point going there, and guilt pronged his chest because he had. The decisions he had made back then had been the right ones and he had no regrets about making them. His sisters had needed him and nothing else had mattered. Then or now.

Shaking off the past, Joe focused on Imogen—on the dark tendrils of hair that had escaped her ponytail and now framed her oval face. On the blue-grey of her eyes, the straight, pert nose and lush, full lips.

'So what happened to those dreams?' he asked quietly. Had they crashed and burned like his?

Picking up her cup, she rested her gaze on his mouth. 'Common sense prevailed. Bills need to be paid...security needs to be ensured. Starving in a garret sounds very romantic, but in real life I like my food too much. So I ended up opting for a PA role. I'm more than happy with that.'

Coffee splashed onto the table as she thunked the cup down, the black droplets pooling on the plastic. Instantly she grabbed a napkin to absorb the liquid.

For a moment Joe was tempted to argue. She didn't look that happy to him. But that really was nothing to do with him.

'Good,' he said instead. 'If you think of anything else to do with Richard let me know. Anything that could give us the edge.'

'I can tell you more about him, if that would help. He's

very generous—almost too much so. He likes throwing his money around and it can come across as a bit in your face, or as if he's showing off. But it's not like that. I think he thinks he has to buy friendship. Reading between the lines, I think he had a pretty rotten childhood. So, yes, he's generous. On the flip side of that he *does* have a bit of a chip on his shoulder, and that can make him take offence easily. He's also a touch eccentric—there's a story about how he actually locked three rival advertising executives in a room together and gave them an hour to come up with a snappy slogan. Said he was fed up with long meetings and endless presentations and statistics.'

Joe drummed his fingers on the table. Clearly the two of them had got on—that would be an advantage. What else could they use?

'Have you been to Paris before?' he asked.

'Nope.'

'Has Graham?'

A frown creased her forehead. 'I'm not sure… Oh, yes, actually he has.' An indecipherable expression flitted across her features. 'He proposed to his wife atop the Eiffel Tower.'

Was it his imagination or was there a quiver of bitterness in her voice?

'Is that the sort of thing that will impress Richard Harvey?'

'Yes, but I don't think there's much we can do about that. Unless, of course, you…?'

'No. I've never proposed to anyone in Paris.'

For a second the memory of his one and only proposal entered his head and he couldn't prevent the bone-deep shudder that went through him. The humiliation of being on bended knee, Leila's look of sheer horror, the violin faltering to a stop in the background… *Whoa. Not going there.*

'But,' he said. 'I *do* think we need to do something to impress Richard. Something that will appeal to his eccentricity more than a lengthy proposal.'

'Such as…?'

'What time are we meeting him?'

'Six p.m.'

Joe looked at his watch. 'So we'll have a few hours when we get there. Let's go to Montmartre.'

Confusion furrowed her brow further. 'Why?'

'Because it will appeal to Richard's sense of the romantic as well. We can tell him we've soaked in the ambience, walked the streets of a place where great art has flourished. And…' He shrugged. 'For a few hours you can live your dream.'

The words sounded way too significant.

'I'll even buy you a beret.'

Live your dream.

Imogen followed Joe across the bustling train station, revelling in the sound of French being spoken around her and inhaling the aroma of croissants and baguettes that was being emitted from patisseries and *boulangeries*. No matter what, she wasn't going to let Steve's actions spoil the next few hours and her chance to see a bit of Paris.

The chance to *live her dream*.

Oh, God. Her eyes snagged on the breadth of Joe's back as he strode through the crowds He had no idea what he was suggesting; if she lived her X-rated dreams she'd be arrested.

Her head whirled as a flutter of nerves rippled her tummy, her thoughts running amok as they made their way through the bustle of the Métro.

Joe hadn't so much as flirted with her, and yet…there was something. Something in the way his eyes rested on her that sent a shiver through her. Something…just something that was making her overheated imagination leap and soar.

Something that was mixing with the anger at Steve that continued to burn inside her…something that was making her want to be different.

Deliberately, she reached up and pulled the pins out of her hair, ran her fingers through it so that it rippled free to her shoulders. She felt Joe stiffen by her side, saw his hand clench around his broad thigh. Astounded by her own daring she oh, so casually allowed her leg to brush against his, revelling in the solid muscle. Then surprise shot out a tendril as a tremor ran through his body.

What if…what if Joe was *attracted* to her? Even a little bit?

Stop it, Imogen.

That way lay madness. Joe McIntyre was a ruthless businessman and her temporary boss. Moreover he was responsible for sacking her friends and colleagues. Worst of all he was considering a buy-out by Ivan Moreton. Joe McIntyre was the enemy, and she'd do well to remember it.

'Our stop,' he said.

They emerged into the late summer sunshine and Imogen tipped her face up and let the rays warm her. It was glorious, and the feel of the cobblestones through her sensible flat navy pumps seemed to send Parisian history straight to her very soul.

Glancing up at Joe, she wondered if the surroundings were affecting him. Somehow he looked different—his mouth a touch less grim, his whole body more relaxed. His sleeves were rolled up and her eyes snagged on his forearms and she gulped. A sudden crazy urge to capture his toned muscular glory on canvas touched her. Montmartre—home to so many artistic greats—must be getting to her.

'OK. Where first?' Joe asked.

She swivelled to look at the imposing outline of the Sacré Coeur, looming on the Paris skyline in its sugar-white beauty. Considered the cemetery where so many artistes were buried. Then there were all the shops, the *tabacs*, the boutiques, the Moulin Rouge, the…'

Yet right now all she could focus on was Joe.

Think, Imogen. Focus.

'Let's get lost in the alleyways—randomly explore. And I've heard of a wonderful fabric shop that is here some-where—maybe we'll find that. Richard would appreci-ate that. If we can I'd love to go the Sacré Coeur as well.'

'Sounds like a plan,' he said as he tugged his dark blue tie off and shoved it into his jacket pocket, then freed the top button of his shirt.

To reveal the bronzed column of his throat.

Licking suddenly parched lips, Imogen knew they had to get moving before she threw her arms around him and pressed her lips to the warmth of his skin. Yet the danger-ous attraction tilted through her, urging her to throw cau-tion to the wind. Be shocking, be different.

Make a total arse of herself.

Any minute now Joe was going to sense how she was feeling, see her quiver with desire, and then mortification would consume her. She'd made enough of a fool of her-self over Steve to last a lifetime.

'This way,' she said brightly, and plunged into an al-leyway, barely aware of the bright colours and bustling crowds.

The key was to keep talking until she'd got her head on straight. Dredging her brain for any information she had on Montmartre, she kept up a flow of conversation. 'Such an amazing place… Did you know there are so many art-ists who lived and worked and are buried here…? Not only artists… Have you heard of Dalida…? Iconic singer…but so tragic… Amazing how many artists are tragic, really…

My father was a big fan of Degas…and Zola… Isn't it so wonderful to be here…? I really feel we are getting the real Montmartre vibes—'

'Imogen.' Joe's deep voice broke into her words. 'Are you OK?'

'Of course. I'm just making conversation.'

'I think you'll find you're making a monologue,' he said.

'Yes, well. It's so super…'

Super? Really, Imogen?

'To be here. We're getting the real Montmartre vibes. I guess I'm a little overexcited.'

'Hardly surprising, really,' he said, and now his rich voice was laced with amusement. 'This is definitely the essence of Montmartre, all right.'

'Huh…?'

Foreboding raised the hair on her arms as she looked round. Oh, crap. Crap. Crappity-crap. Garish neon signs vied with more artistic depictions, but it was abundantly clear exactly where they were.

The entire street was filled with sex shops.

CHAPTER FOUR

NOW WHAT?

Soon enough she'd be able to boil a kettle on her cheeks—not that a kettle would be easy to come by in a sex shop.

This was the stuff of nightmares; they couldn't just have found a street full of museums, could they? Or artists sketching people? Oh, no! Or this couldn't have happened when she was with Mel. Or on her own. With *anyone* other than Joe McIntyre.

Her nerves jangled with irritation as he looked round with an interest he didn't even bother to hide before turning his gaze back on her.

Damn the blush that still burnt her cheeks, and damn her prudish upbringing that had left her believing that sex was something dangerous.

Not that she blamed her mother; Eva Lorrimer had fallen prey to lust and then fallen pregnant—an event that had thoroughly derailed her life. She'd ended up married to a penniless artist she'd had nothing in common with—a man she'd considered beneath her socially and intellectually whom she had never forgiven. Any more than she'd forgiven herself.

Little wonder she'd drummed into Imogen the need never to let herself be dazzled by looks or taken in by 'the physical side of things'. Her mother would have hustled her out with here, hands over her eyes. But Eva wasn't here.

Plus it was ridiculous, really—this insane feeling of awkwardness. Looking round, it was more than clear to her that no one else was embarrassed. Couples strolled with their arms wrapped round each other's waists, stopping to look into windows. A group of women whose pink bunny rabbit outfits indicated that they were without doubt on a hen party laughed raucously, the noise carrying on the afternoon air. Chic single women, debonair single men, groups of chatting tourists all smiled, sauntered on completely at ease. Whereas *she* stood here like some prim and proper maiden from Victorian times.

The amused look that Joe gave her didn't help one bit, ruffling her self-annoyance into a desire to…to…to what? Kick him. *Very mature, Imo.*

'I take it you didn't plan on visiting this particular bit of the district.'

'No.'

'Come on, then. I think if we double back down that alleyway there we should hit a *different* type of shop and then it shouldn't be difficult to find the Sacré Coeur.'

Imogen hauled in a breath and stiffened her spine. 'Now that we're here I think we should check one out.'

Joe's brown eyes glittered with surprise and something else—perhaps a flash of discomfort. *Ha!* Maybe he wasn't as man-of-the-world as he appeared to be.

'You sure?'

Double *ha*! She was right. His body was ever so slightly rigid and his voice had a hint of clenched jaw and gritted teeth about it.

So now she knew that he was feeling awkward too, the sensible thing to do would be to get the hell off this street. *Sensible.*

The word grated on her soul.

She was sick of being sensible. She had oh, so sensibly picked an oh, so sensible man—using her über-sensible tick list—and look where it had got her. Well, stuff it. Sensible Imogen could take a hike. Not for ever, but just for a while. Temporary New Imogen was going to take over and things were going to be different.

The unfamiliar spark of rebellion took hold and took over her vocal cords.

'Of course I'm sure. Why shouldn't I be? There's nothing wrong in having an interest. A *healthy* interest in… you know…' Imogen closed her eyes in silent despair. Had she said that?

'I do know,' he said, and suddenly the atmosphere thickened. The buzz of French chatter, the sound of the church bells all dimmed. Everything faded and all Imogen was aware of was the look in Joe's eyes as he stepped towards her. So close that she could smell that tantalising male aroma, the underlying sandalwood. So close that if she lifted a hand she would be able to place her fingers on the width of his chest and feel the beat of his heart.

Whoa!

They both stepped back at exactly the same second and Imogen gave a slightly shaky laugh, horribly aware that her legs were feeling more than a touch jellified.

Joe rubbed the back of his neck and his face was neutralised, all emotion cleared. 'Lead the way,' he said.

Joe knew this was a bad idea; he was having enough issues keeping his attraction for Imogen leashed. Entering through the portals of a sex shop with her probably wasn't going to help—not so much because of the merchandise but more because he sensed that Imogen was bubbling with…*something.* She had been all day and certainly was now; there was undoubtedly an emotional maelstrom brewing and he wasn't at all sure he wanted to be caught up in its wake.

'This one,' Imogen said, pointing towards a large well-lit store that looked like an emporium or even a supermarket.

Joe followed her through the doors into the spacious

shop and nearly crashed straight into her back as Imogen came to an abrupt halt. Moving next to her, he glanced down at her and saw her eyes widen, but before he could say anything a shop assistant crossed the floor.

In his forties, the man had a discreet charming smile, dark blond hair and an urbane manner. *'Bonjour,'* he said courteously. *'Anglais?'*

Joe nodded. *'Oui, monsieur. Je parle français, mais—'* He broke off. Maybe Imogen did speak French. 'Do you speak French?' he asked.

A shake of her head served as her answer; evidently the merchandise was still rendering her speechless.

The man smiled. 'It is not a problem,' he said. 'I speak English. My name is Jean and I am here to help. Is there anything in particular the two of you are looking for? Something to spice up—?'

Imogen's head snapped round. 'We aren't together.'

'Apologies. You just have the look of—'

'Colleagues,' Imogen intercepted. 'We are here to… research…for a friend…who is…um…writing a book on erotica.'

Jean swept his gaze over them. 'I comprehend completely,' he said, his voice smooth. 'You are enquiring for a friend. Many people do that. So, you must let me show you around to make sure your…friend…gets a proper overview of passion. I shall show you items that can enhance pleasure.'

Joe felt a shudder run through Imogen's body and wondered what she was thinking. Was she imagining herself in the throes of passion—? Oh, hell—*her* thoughts weren't the problem here. His, however, were. Images branded his retina. His body wasn't interested in anything that this shop could offer—his body knew that all it needed was Imogen's touch. In fact any enhancement and he'd probably go up in flames.

So perhaps a guided tour was preferable to walking round just with Imogen.

'*Merci*, Jean. Much appreciated.'

'This way.' Jean stepped forward.

'Why did you agree?' Imogen whispered.

'Why did you say we were researching for a friend? If that were true we would *want* a tour.'

No way was he explaining *his* need for a chaperon.

'Now, here we have the lingerie. Come closer—touch… feel.'

Jean motioned to Imogen and after a second's hesitation she stepped forward and fingered the deep midnight-black confection. 'Oh…'

Joe bit back a groan at her reaction. Her gasp was soft, yet so appreciative as her slender fingers stroked the material.

'It's so sensual,' she murmured. 'Is it pure silk or…or a mixture?'

For a second Jean looked surprised, and then his face cleared. 'Ah, you are a woman who likes texture and feel. This is a blend of silk and satin, but we also have other fabrics. Cashmere…soft suede. Perhaps for you the blindfold would be a good thing?'

Imogen dropped the lingerie and jumped backwards. 'Um…I'm not sure…'

But Jean was in full swing as he led them inexorably over to a section that was devoted to an extensive range of blindfolds. 'You see, to be deprived of sight lifts the anticipation and allows the other senses to come into play.'

The audible hitch of her breath, the flush that tinged her high cheekbones, told Joe all he needed to know. Imogen was wondering exactly what it would be like to be blindfolded—and, heaven help him, *he* wanted to be there when she explored that particular fantasy.

'I am sure,' Jean said smoothly, 'that your friend would be interested in this.'

'Friend?' Imogen flushed even redder and then nodded. 'Yes, absolutely. This is all very helpful. Isn't it, Joe?'

There was a certain part of his anatomy that would undoubtedly disagree.

Her elbow in his ribs prompted his vocal cords and demonstrated exactly how close they were standing. 'Yup. Our friend will be very interested in all this.'

Jean beamed. 'Then let's keep going. Down here is the costume aisle. You have the nurse costumes, the superhero, the…'

Aisle followed aisle, until finally Jean came to a halt.

'So this has been helpful?'

Joe stepped forward. 'Amazingly so. Thank you, Jean.'

'We'll be sure to recommend our friend visits here,' Imogen chimed in.

Minutes later they exited the shop, and Joe inhaled the Parisian air as they started walking in the late-afternoon sun, heading towards the Sacré Coeur.

Imogen stared down at the ground as she walked, presumably shell-shocked by the mass of information she had accrued.

'I can't believe we did that,' she said.

Neither could he. What had he been thinking? Checking out a sex shop was hardly a work-related activity, however he spun it. Time to regroup.

'Let's stop for coffee and check out a map to find that fabric place you mentioned.'

'OK. Good idea.'

He led the way into a small café and sat down at a scarred wooden table. A few minutes later, espresso in one hand and a map in the other, he expelled a sigh of relief. Control restored.

Until he glanced at her, took in the way she twirled a tendril of hair round her finger as she gazed at him almost speculatively.

'What?' he said.

'I'm not sure I can ask,' she said.

He snorted. 'We just spent half an hour in a sex shop with a man extolling the virtues of a Power Stallion vibrator. Right now you can ask me anything.'

She stared at him for a moment and her lips tipped up in a smile. 'I wish you could have seen your face when he said it still wasn't quite the same as the real thing.'

He grinned. 'I imagine my expression was pretty much a mirror image of yours when he explained what a g-wand does.'

Imogen giggled—a full-on, proper fit of giggles—and as he watched her features scrunch up in mirth he couldn't help himself. A sudden chuckle fell from his lips and developed into laughter. The kind that came straight from the belly. The sort of laughter he hadn't experienced for a while—not since his sisters had taken off travelling.

'I can't believe it really happened,' Imogen said breathlessly. 'Poor Jean. We should have bought something, really.'

Lord—she looked so beautiful when she laughed. Her face was so alive, her dark hair highlighted by the sunshine filtering through the window. An intense spike of desire pierced his chest, and the urge to lean across the polished wood of the table and cover her delectable mouth with his own was almost overwhelming.

Gripping the edge of the table, he forced himself to remain still, all inclination to mirth gone.

Her blue-grey eyes met his and her laughter ceased abruptly.

The silence thickened and her lips parted as her breathing quickened. Joe's brain was scrambled. Conversation—he had to find something to say before sheer momentum tilted him towards her.

'So, what were you going to ask?'

Imogen blinked, as if his words were reaching her through a haze of desire. 'It doesn't matter. Really.'

'No, go ahead.' Surely she grasped that they *had* to talk—use their lips to form words, not anything else.

'All those things in the shop… Do you think they're important in a relationship?'

OK. This wasn't the topic he'd been hoping for. Damn it, couldn't she have been wondering about the weather, or French politics, or his opinion on the socioeconomic state of Britain or something?

'Would you like your girlfriend to come home dressed as Wonder Woman, wielding a whip?' she continued.

'I don't have a girlfriend.' As answers went it was a cop-out, but as questions went hers hadn't exactly been social chitchat.

'Hypothetically?'

'Not hypothetically either. I'm not really a relationship type of guy.'

'So you're celibate?' Imogen raised a hand to her mouth as pink stained her cheeks. 'Hell. Sorry. I really did *not* mean to say that.'

'Don't worry—and, no, I'm not celibate. I just don't do relationships.'

'So what *do* you do? One-night stands only?'

For a moment he was tempted to duck the question, but a strange defensiveness tightened his grip around his coffee cup. 'Yes.'

'Oh. So, then…um…would you mind if your bedroom partner was into all that stuff?'

'I wouldn't have a problem exploring the idea of using some of the things Jean showed us, but I certainly don't expect or want all my bedmates to come accessorised with a whip or a latex uniform.'

'But would you *prefer* a partner who wanted to explore those ideas?'

'If we're going to have this conversation—' and heaven only knew why they were '—then I need to know why we're having it.'

'It's…' For a second she stared down at her coffee. 'Research.'

'Research for what?'

'I was wondering if I should…well…maybe pick up a few items from Jean's arsenal.'

'That's something you would need to discuss with *your* bedroom partner.'

'Given my current bed partner is a cuddly rabbit that's seen better days, that's probably not going to work. That's why I'm asking you. For a general opinion.'

'I don't think turn-ons can be boiled down into a general formula, Imogen. Everyone's rules of attraction are different.'

Imogen sighed. 'I guess I've just never thought that sexual attraction was particularly important in a relationship.'

Joe frowned. How could a woman so clearly made for the bedroom think sexual attraction was unimportant?

'That probably explains the rabbit situation,' he said.

Clearly not the right thing to say.

Imogen's eyes narrowed. 'You're saying I'm single because I don't believe sex is the be-all and end-all to life?'

'I'm saying sexual attraction is a key component to a relationship.'

'What makes *you* an expert? You just said you don't do relationships.'

'I don't. But I *do* do sexual attraction, and I can vouch for it being an important thing.'

'Sure. But there are other things that are way more important. Kindness, loyalty, shared goals, a sense of humour, being good parent material. They all rate way higher than sexual attraction on my tick-list.' Her voice vibrated with absolute belief.

'Tick-list?' *She had a tick-list?* 'You have an actual, for real list of requirements? Manly chest? Sizeable bank balance? A yen to walk down the aisle.'

He was honest-to-God fascinated.

'Chest size irrelevant,' she said.

Though he couldn't help but notice her gaze linger on his pecs with perhaps a hint of regret.

'Moderate rather than sizeable savings account to demonstrate that security is important to him. And, yes, I need him to be pro marriage. And kids. I want financial security and whilst I'm happy to share my salary I need a partner who pulls their weight.' Her voice had a steely ring Joe usually heard in a corporate boardroom not a bedroom. Any minute now she'd give him a PowerPoint presentation. 'I want a man who wants children, who will be a wonderful dad who puts his children before himself.'

'So what do you do? Sit every eligible man down, ask for a copy of his bank statement and make him write an essay on his opinion of a white picket fence?'

'Of course not.' Against the odds her eyes narrowed further. 'But, yes, I do need to know whether we have long-term compatibility. So of course I do an assessment.'

'You don't think that's a bit clinical?' To say nothing of a touch kooky.

'No more clinical than only having one-night stands to serve a bodily function.'

The disdain in her voice touched a nerve.

'A one-night stand is about way more than bodily functions.'

'If you say so…'

Her nose wrinkled in distaste and defensiveness rose within him.

'I do. It's about passion and chemistry and spark.'

He allowed his gaze to linger on her mouth, heard her breath catch in the slender column of her throat.

'When the scent of the other person turns you on, when the idea of touching them becomes consuming, when all you want to do is pull them into your arms and kiss them.'

Her tongue snaked out to moisten the bow of her lips and his willpower snapped. Maybe he could show her what she was dismissing with such contempt.

'A bit like now,' he growled.

And in one movement he hitched his chair around the curve of the wooden table and cupped her jaw in his hands, expelled a sigh at the silken texture of her skin beneath his fingers. He ran his thumb over the fullness of her lower lip, saw the quiver run through her body.

As he covered her lips with his own, Joe was dimly aware that this was a bad, *bad* idea—but then Imogen's taste, her scent, her warmth eradicated all vestige of thought. All he wanted was to plunder the softness of her coffee-scented lips as they parted to allow him access.

Her tongue tentatively stroked his, and as she moaned into his mouth he was lost. He tangled his fingers in her smooth glossy hair as she twined her arms around his neck; her fingers brushed his nape and desire jolted through him.

'Closer,' she murmured, and he slid his hands over her shoulders and down, spanned her slender waist and pulled her onto his lap.

Who knew how long they remained, lips locked, lost in sheer pleasure? Until the clink and clatter of plates, the whir of the coffee machine penetrated his brain. What the hell was he doing? Melded against someone tantamount to being an employee. Someone whose job he had the power to take. Someone who could be trying to influence him to protect not just her own job but other people's as well.

Hell and damnation.

Pulling backwards, he broke the kiss and she gave a small mewl of protest, her eyes pools of desire clouded with confusion.

Her breathing as ragged as his, she scrambled off him and stood, one hand gripping the table for support. 'I…I…'

Joe hauled in air and willed his pulse-rate to slow down and his brain to move into gear. Imogen did not look like a woman out to seduce him for gain; she looked as shell-shocked as he felt. Surely that couldn't be simulated?

Regardless… 'That was a mistake,' he said flatly.

Yet she looked so damn desirable still, with her hair dishevelled, her lips swollen from his kiss, that it took all his willpower to remain seated.

Chill, Joe. It was a kiss. One kiss. Even if it had been the kiss of all kisses it was not a deal-breaker. 'Never Mix Business with Pleasure' was still Rule Number One.

Yes, he'd erred; he'd let the line between professional and personal fuzz. Given Imogen a few hours to live the dream, agreed to visit a sex shop, shared laughter, discussed sex. Time to redraw that line in permanent marker. Of the fluorescent kind.

'A mistake that we need to put behind us.' He glanced at his watch. 'We've got a couple of hours. Let's put them to good use and visit some places that will impress Richard Harvey.' As opposed to a sex shop.

Imogen nodded, tugged the edges of her jacket together and smoothed down her trousers, visibly pulling herself together. 'I think we should find the fabric shop, visit the cemetery and go to the Sacré Coeur.'

'Done.'

Imogen walked up and up and up the calf-wrenching steps towards the top of the glorious domed cathedral. She welcomed the pain—welcomed even more the legitimate reason for her heart to pound against her ribcage.

As the sun struck the blinding white of the travertine walls she was dazzled—not just by the rays but by the sheer dizzying possibilities of life.

She knew how she *should* be feeling: thoroughly ashamed with herself. She'd kissed a man who was her boss, her enemy, the wrecker of her friends' and colleagues' lives. Joe had spoken the truth: the kiss *had* been a mistake.

But it had also been earth-shattering. She'd never experienced one like it and her body still fizzed with the sheer joy of it. Apparently lust trumped principles. But who would have thought a kiss could be so incredible? How could she regret a kiss like that?

Apprehension prickled her skin. *Take care, Imo.* Perhaps this was how her mother had felt all those years before—beguiled by Jonathan Lorrimer's looks and charm. And look what had happened there.

Not that Joe was remotely charming, nor making any attempt to beguile her. In fact he appeared to have erased the kiss from his memory banks.

Their whole trip around the fabric store and their entire tour of the museum had been achieved civilly enough— Joe had asked intelligent questions about the fabrics, observed the paintings in the museum with genuine appreciation—but gone was the man who had laughed with her and wreaked such magic with his kiss. *This* man was the consummate professional, with his tie back round his neck as if that could restore professional equilibrium.

Currently Imogen would have settled for any sort of equilibrium. Even now the nape of her neck tingled. Every molecule of her body was hyper-aware of the strength of him just behind her on the narrow stairway as they approached the summit.

Her breath caught as she looked down over the awe-inspiring vista of Paris. The Eiffel Tower jutted above the rooftops of thousands of differently shaped buildings, all glinting in the late-afternoon sun. It made her feel dizzy, different, infused with wonder.

'It's incredible…'

'Yes.'

Had his gaze lingered on her face for a heartbeat before he'd turned to stare out at the panorama?

Ridiculous. He was talking about the view, for heaven's sake! She had to get some perspective. They'd shared a kiss. Big deal. Now they had to return to normal. Joe equalled Big Bad Boss. Imogen equalled Employee. She needed to concentrate on her job.

'Have you seen it before?' she asked. There. Perfect. Normal civil conversation.

'Yes.' As if realising the brevity of the syllable, he continued, 'I came with my sisters once.'

'Really?' It was strange to imagine Joe in family mode.

'Really.' A smile touched his lips—a genuine one. 'I'm not sure they appreciated the glory of the scenery. They were fourteen and more interested in the glory of French boys.'

His lips pressed together, as though he regretted sharing even that much personal information.

A glance at his watch and, 'We need to go.'

Guilt prodded her as she scuttled after him through the tourist crowd. She'd completely lost track of time—hadn't given work a single thought since they'd got on the Métro. All she'd thought about was Joe. Oh, and sex. In conjunction.

As their taxi screeched and sped through the Paris traffic Imogen squeezed her hands into fists and focused. The hours for living the dream were over and it was time to concentrate on reality and the need to wow Richard. If only her body would stop with the snap, crackle and pop…

The taxi glided to a stop and she climbed out, stood on the pavement whilst Joe paid the driver. The street teemed with chicly dressed chattering women and casually dressed men. Elegance mixed with gesticulation and passion, and for a minute Imogen wished with all her heart that she was in Paris with a lover.

Joe.

Delusional, Imo.

'Let's go,' she said, and they wended their way through the throng into the warmly lit interior of a bar.

Small and intimate, its tables glowed golden in the muted light from retro lamps and the candles that dotted the embrasures in the wax-dripped wall.

A bar curved down one side of the room, behind which there was a bewildering array of bottles and an old-fashioned cash register that evoked images of a Paris of decades before. The soft strains of jazz filled the evening air, reminding Imogen of the sheer thrill of being in the romantic capital of the world.

'Over here.'

Peering through the throng, Imogen spotted Richard and Crystal sitting in a corner booth, a pitcher of delicate pink liquid on the table in front of them.

Happiness was evident in the glow of their smiles, the linking of their fingers as they both rose to their feet. Richard looked younger than she remembered, his salt-and-pepper hair longer, his whole stance more relaxed.

No doubt that was Crystal's influence. In her late thirties, she radiated a serene timeless beauty and her glance at her husband was soft with love. For them Paris was a truly romantic getaway, and envy tugged at Imogen's heartstrings.

Forcing a smile to her face, she stepped forward and greeted the couple, introduced Joe.

'Good to meet you, Joe,' Richard said. 'Sit—order whatever you like. On me. I recommend the Vieux Carré cocktail. Cognac, sweet vermouth, rye and Benedictine, with a dash of Angostura bitters.'

'Sounds good to me,' Joe said.

'Me too,' Imogen agreed.

Once they were seated, with their drinks in front of them, Richard smiled at Imogen. 'Isn't Steve accompanying you on this trip? I thought you'd take advantage of the chance for a romantic getaway?'

Next to her Joe stiffened for a second, his movements jerky as he picked his glass up.

'Maybe give him the opportunity to pop the question if he hasn't already, eh?'

Mortification encased her body as her cheeks heated to no doubt a tomato-red. Memories came of how she had gushed to Richard about her belief that she and Steve were so suited, so compatible, so together.

She had been truly delusional.

Now she would have to admit that Steve had left her for his ex and was going to marry her. Well, call her a great fat fibber but she couldn't do it—couldn't bear to see the pity in Richard Harvey's eyes.

'He couldn't make it,' she said, ignoring the snap of Joe's head, sure she could feel his look boring through her temple.

'That's a real shame,' Crystal said. 'We were hoping to meet him.'

Richard turned to Joe. 'Did *you* bring a significant other half with you?'

'No. *I'm* a single man.'

The older man sighed, and then shrugged. 'Then I suppose the best thing will be for you both to stay in the apartment.'

Huh? The words of confession Imogen had been preparing withered on her tongue. Trepidation tiptoed down her spine as she picked up her glass and forced herself to sip rather than gulp.

'What apartment would that be?' she managed.

Richard smiled. 'Well, as you know, Crystal and I have

bought a place in Paris and want it done up. I could go to someone over here, but I'd prefer to use either you or Graham. So I've come up with a plan.'

Oh, hell; this plan was going to be a Harvey Humdinger—Imogen just knew it.

'Sounds intriguing,' Joe murmured.

'I've rented two romantic Parisian apartments,' Richard explained. 'One for Graham and his wife and one was meant to be for Imogen and Steve—though now it's for you two. You stay there tonight. Then on Monday morning I want a two-page proposal on how you would design the interior of a four-bedroom, three-bathroom Parisian apartment. I'll make my decision based on that.'

'How does that sound?' Crystal asked.

'That sounds like a challenge Langley will be more than happy to accept,' Joe said.

Come on, Imogen. She could do the whole gibbering wreck thing later. Right now wasn't the time.

Raising her glass, she summoned a smile that she could only hope denoted calm, professional confidence. 'I'll drink to that.'

'Excellent,' Richard said. He reached into his pocket and pushed a set of keys across the table. 'Here are the keys to 'Lovers' Tryst.'

Of course. What else could it be called?

Joe and Imogen—off to Lovers' Tryst for the night. Dear Lord.

Panic bubbled in her tummy, and yet a thoroughly misplaced anticipation strummed her veins.

CHAPTER FIVE

IMOGEN SWEPT A sideways glance across the limo that Richard had insisted they use and shifted on the seat, nerves jangling. Joe's whole body pulsed with contained anger and had done ever since they had said their goodbyes to Richard and Crystal. It wasn't her fault that Richard had come up with this mad idea, so she could only assume that his irritation was at the situation—not her.

Sod it. The brooding silence was getting old. 'So,' she said brightly, 'isn't it generous of Richard to say he'll pay for any clothes and things that we need to purchase? And to have booked us a table at one of the poshest restaurants in Paris?' She glanced down at herself. 'Do you think this is all right to wear to eat in a French restaurant? Probably not.'

'It doesn't make any difference to me whether you wear a sack,' he said, the words rasping in the regulated air of the limo. 'So don't waste your time or Richard's money on a seduction outfit.'

'What?' Confusion tangled her vocal cords. 'I don't understand.'

'I don't like being played, Imogen.'

'Still not with you.'

'I don't trade business favours for sexual ones.'

'*Excuse* me?'

'The kiss.'

Her neck cracked as she swivelled on the plush leather seat to face his grim expression. The dusk had harshened the angles of his face further. 'Are you for real? You think that was for *business* reasons?'

'You wouldn't be the first to try it. You said yourself you would do anything to save Langley. Maybe you're hoping to persuade me to drop the buy-out plan, give your friends their jobs back.' He leant back against the padded leather. 'So if you had seduction plans for later cancel them.'

'Believe me, Joe, I'd rather seduce...' Hell she couldn't think of anyone low enough. 'Ivan...'

'Maybe that's your plan B. Though I can't help feeling sorry for that poor sap of a boyfriend you've got at home, waiting to propose. The man who satisfies your crazy tick-list. Does Steve *know* you go round kissing people in cafés? Sitting on their laps and—'

'Stop!'

Imogen wondered if it were possible to explode with rage. If so, she damn well hoped she took Joe with her. Anger ignited, heated her veins. How *dared* he?

'You arrogant, stupid schmuck! For your information, Steve and I split up six weeks ago.'

He snorted. 'More lies, Imogen? Why didn't you tell Richard?'

'Because I felt such a damn fool. I raved about Steve to Richard, about him being The One. I was too embarrassed to admit I was wrong.'

As the limo glided to a stop outside a shopping mall tears of sheer rage and mortification threatened. How could Joe tarnish a kiss that had made her blood sing and her head spin? Made her feel attractive and desirable and wanted? Palliated the sting of Steve's parting words?

Now it turned out he believed she had engineered that kiss because she was a gold-digger, a spy or a cheat. Good grief—if she wasn't so furious she'd laugh. Because one thing she knew: Joe had been just as much into that kiss as she had.

'I think you're forgetting something, here. That *you* kissed *me*!'

'Imogen…'

'Just leave it, Joe.' She shoved the car door open, nearly tumbling the chauffeur over as he waited to open the door for her, and set off across the car park, her rage spiking further as she marched, feet pounding the tarmac, and realised he wasn't damn well even going to follow her.

Fine.

Anger heated her veins, seethed and simmered as her brain formulated a plan.

She'd show him. She'd show him exactly what he was missing. There wasn't a cat's chance in hell she'd seduce him, but she was damn well going to make him wish she would.

Sanity tried to point out that maybe Joe had been a little misled by the fib she'd told Richard. But that wasn't the point! He could just have *asked* her before jumping to such insulting, stupid conclusions.

An hour later Imogen stared at her reflection, relieved that rage still buoyed her because she knew otherwise there was no way in heaven or hell she would be able to carry this off.

The dress was…outrageous. In a good way. It managed to scream seduction whilst hollering elegance. Black see-through gauze featured, fluttering to mid-thigh and covering her chest, whilst allowing tantalising glimpses of the black corset-like bit underneath. Shells striped the dress in a fun, flirty line, and the whole look was complemented by the strappiest high-heeled shoes imaginable. Delicate leather lines crisscrossed her feet, cool and seductive against her skin.

'*C'est magnifique!*' the sales assistant exclaimed, clapping her hands together.

'*Merci bien.*'

To her own surprise she didn't feel even a smidgeon of self-consciousness as she walked through the mall. Instead she fizzed with a sheer intoxicating vitality, every sense heightened and fuelled by the attention she garnered.

Joe was leaning back against the limo, arms folded, the breadth of his shoulders somehow accentuated by the length of the car. His white shirt had been swapped for a black one, with the top button undone to reveal a triangle of tanned skin that tantalised her gaze. He was intent on his phone screen, and a frown slashed his forehead.

Anticipation whispered in her stomach as she neared him and he looked up. The temptation to punch the air at his expression nearly overwhelmed her but she restrained it. Instead she savoured every second of his dropped jaw, every shade of heat that glittered in his brown eyes as they swept over her, lingering in appreciation as he stepped towards her.

Her brain gave out conflicting orders—*step towards him, move backwards, turn and run*. Grinding her molars, she adhered her stilettoed feet to the tarmac of the car park and faced him. He was so close she could smell the tang of masculinity, the scent of arousal. Her muscles ached with a need to reach out and touch him, to trace a finger along that V of skin, to unbutton his shirt and…

No! The plan was to show him what he was missing— not to offer herself up on a plate, thereby confirming all his insulting, overbearing assumptions.

'You ready for the restaurant?' she asked, keeping her voice casual with a supreme effort of will. 'I figure it will be pretty upmarket, so I want to look my best. You never know. As you're not available I may get lucky and find some loaded French sex god to seduce instead.'

She slapped her palm to her forehead.

'Oh, yes. I forgot. I'm *not* here with some cunning plan

to seduce anyone. I'm here to work. To come up with a proposal for Richard and Crystal.'

Joe stepped backwards, leant against the car and raised his eyebrows. 'You can hardly blame me for jumping to the conclusions I did.'

'Wrong. I can *totally* blame you. You could have asked first. You know—like, *Imogen, I'm a bit confused. Who is Steve?*'

'OK.' Folding his arms, he met her gaze. 'Imogen, I'm a bit confused. Who is Steve?'

'I told you. He is my *ex*-boyfriend. I am a free agent, and that kiss earlier wasn't about me being out to get anything or me being unfaithful to anyone.'

'So what *was* it about?'

'You tell me.'

His heated gaze swept over her body and then he straightened up, the glint in his eyes doused. 'It was a moment of insanity,' he said. 'And I apologise. For being so unprofessional. How about we put the whole episode behind us and move forward? Truce?'

What could she say? His voice was sincere, his gaze direct. 'Truce,' she agreed.

The twitch of his lips was a surprise as he gestured towards her. 'I take it that dress was chosen with the express purpose of torturing me?'

'Absolutely. Is it working?'

'Yes.'

Why, oh, why did he have to smile? A devastating smile sinful enough to make her hair curl. Oh, God. Perhaps this whole idea hadn't been so brilliant after all—especially as Joe wasn't playing the part she'd allotted him. Her tummy churned as she tried to work out what the hell was going on. Wondered if Joe had any idea either.

He opened the limo door for her and she slid inside, pulling her stomach muscles in so as not to so much as brush against him before scooting all the way across the leather seat.

Clamping her knees together, she shoved away the realisation that short and see-through, whilst effective, was also…well, short and see-through. From somewhere she had to muster the light sabre of professionalism. Hadn't she said she was here to work? Now would be an excellent moment to do exactly that.

'So,' she said. 'What do you think about Richard's idea of a two-page proposal?'

'I think you were right. Richard Harvey is a touch eccentric. But his idea has its merits. We'll have a quick decision for the minimum outlay of time.' He paused. 'I do realise he's thrown you in at the deep end, though. I'm thinking about calling Belinda off a project so that she can come and look at the apartment.'

Joe's words were as effective as a bucket of ice, dousing elation in reality. How stupid was she? It hadn't even occurred to her that *she* wouldn't be the one to put together the proposal. Forget stupid and substitute nonsensical. Her job at Langley was as a PA—sure, she'd dabbled in interior design, but Belinda had proper qualifications and expertise and was the obvious choice to go up against Graham.

Richard had asked for her presence, but he hadn't specified that Imogen worked on the proposal. She was just a point of contact and she should have realised that herself. If she hadn't been too busy living in some sort of fantasyland.

All too aware of Joe's gaze on her face, she looked out of the window, not wanting him to read the hurt or the sheer embarrassment that was no doubt etched there, relieved when the limo pulled to a stop.

'I'll text Belinda from the restaurant.'

It was all for the best. Did she *really* want the responsibility of going up against Graham? Having to face Peter's disappointment and the knowledge that she'd let Langley down if or rather *when* she didn't succeed? Far better to stay ensconced in her comfort zone.

'She's perfect for the proposal.'

Tension pounded Joe's temples as he followed Imogen into the restaurant and nodded automatically at the *maître d'*, who swooped towards them majestically, his gold-braided jacket a perfect fit with all the grandeur of the baroque theme.

Not that Joe cared about the gold and gilt that abounded, or the ornate mirrors on the stone walls, or even the wrought-iron chandeliers that glinted with the ambience of wealth.

Right now he was too busy questioning the swirl and whirl of emotions that Imogen had unleashed inside him. Anger at himself rebounded against a small and unfamiliar sense of panic. There was the ever growing problem of their attraction, not helped by the tantalising torment of her dress. But worse than that was the way his chest had panged at the quickly veiled hurt in her eyes when he'd suggested Belinda.

Realising that the *maître d'* still hovered, he shook the thought away. 'We have a reservation. Made by Richard Harvey,' he said.

The *maître d'* smiled his dignified approval and gestured to a black-suited waiter with a gold tie. 'This is Marcel. He will look after your table. Marcel, please take Miss Lorrimer and her companion to the table Mr Harvey requested for them.'

Joe gave in to temptation and placed his palm on the small of Imogen's back to steer her, his flesh tingling with warmth and an unexpected sense of possession. Just what he needed—more unfamiliar emotions that didn't make sense.

He eyed the table and further misgivings tingled his already frazzled nerve-endings. The table was... The word *intimate* sprang to mind. The kind of table for lovers, not colleagues—the type where you sat at adjacent angles so your knees pressed together, so it was easy to place your hand on your partner's thigh, indulge in a little footsie. The handy pillar would allow or even encourage canoodling.

He suddenly remembered that the gleaming candlelit table had been originally intended for *Steve* and Imogen.

Bloody wonderful.

Marcel seated them and then beamed. 'Mr Harvey has made a selection for you, but he's asked me to tell you first in case you have any allergies.'

Joe allowed the list of exquisite dishes to wash over him; the only relevant thing here was the length of the damn menu. They would be here for *hours*. On the other hand that might well be better than whatever Lovers' Tryst had to hold.

Right now it was time to get a handle on the situation, get a grip of said handle and start steering. Whatever the menu, this was a business dinner.

'That sounds fine. But I'll stick to water rather than wine.'

'It sounds *incredible*,' Imogen interpolated. 'Please make sure that you let Mr Harvey know how much we appreciate all this. And water for me as well, please.'

The waiter bowed, turned and glided across the restaurant floor, leaving them alone. No, not alone. Yet despite the fact that the restaurant was full, and the hum and buzz of conversation filled the air, Joe had the ridiculous impression that he and Imogen were in their own private space.

Imogen darted a glance at him and then reached down for her bag. 'I'll try Belinda now.'

'Is that what *you* want to do?' he asked, rubbing the back of his neck.

A frown creased her forehead as she moistened her lips.
'It makes sense.'

As he forced himself not to linger on her glossy lips it
occurred to him that *nothing* made sense—and that was
the problem. She'd got him so damn distracted that he'd let
the personal and the business line fuzz. *Again*. He couldn't
tell whether he wanted Belinda to come and look at the
apartment because it was best for Langley or because Belinda would provide them with a chaperon. Didn't know
if he wanted to allow Imogen to do the proposal because
that was the right thing for Langley or because he wanted
to assuage the hurt that had flashed across her eyes.

Enough.

Time to apply logic.

'I'm not sure it does,' he said as he drummed his fingers on the snow-white tablecloth. 'The impression I got
was that Richard wants *you* to do it. I also believe that you
understand how his mind works. We're up against a time
limit. And Belinda is flat-out on other projects.'

There was a pause as she looked down at the bread roll
she was crumbling into tiny pieces. 'But I'm a PA. I have
no qualifications in interior design—or advertising and
marketing.'

'But this is coming up with a concept. Isn't that exactly
what you did for Richard's bathrooms?'

'Well, yes. But that was after we'd won the contract.
And if Peter hadn't liked my ideas he'd have nixed them.
There's a whole lot more riding on this.'

'Is that what's scaring you?'

Her fingers stilled, her head coming up as her eyes narrowed. 'It was your idea to bring in Belinda.'

Joe shook his head. 'I acknowledged that Richard was
asking you to take on a lot and said I was *thinking* about
bringing Belinda in. I haven't made a decision.'

'Oh.'

'So, do you think you can pull this off?'

She hesitated, her features creased into worried lines as she manoeuvred the crumbs into a line. 'It's just such a big responsibility. What if I let you down?'

Watching the play of light over her features, he was gripped by the urge to reassure her, to tell her that of *course* she wouldn't, to reach out and cup the delicate curve of her jaw.

Instead, 'There are no guarantees, Imogen. It's the risk you take. For what it's worth, I think you have a better shot at it than Belinda.'

'You do? You think I can pull this off?'

'Yes.'

'For real?'

'For real.'

Her face lit up and her lips curved in a genuine smile that constricted his lungs.

'I've seen your work and I've seen your rapport with Richard. I think that's key. So, yes, I think you can do it. But if you feel more comfortable calling in Belinda that's fine too.'

With a swoop of her hand she swept the crumbs into a small pile and nodded. 'I'll do it. And I'll give it my very best shot. I promise.'

Joe lifted his glass as relief trickled over him—they were back in *business*. His gut told him that using Imogen was the right decision.

'It's a plan,' he said.

'Thank you...'

Leaning forward, she placed a hand on his forearm, her touch sparking awareness. A citrus burst of shampoo, a tendril of black hair tickled his nose as she placed her lips in a fleeting caress against his cheek.

'For believing in me.'

CHAPTER SIX

BIG MISTAKE. FROM the second she slanted her body so close to his Imogen knew she might as well be juggling dynamite. His toned forearm tensed under her fingers and as her lips brushed the six o'clock stubble of his jaw need shivered through her.

The sensible thing to do would be to pull away, but the urge to nuzzle his skin, to take the opportunity to inhale that Joe scent, was nigh on overwhelming. Adrenalin swept through her tummy in a wave—this man wanted her as much as she wanted him, he believed in her, and he was so damn close that suddenly it seemed mad to fight this attraction. In this second she couldn't even remember why they were.

His body stilled, and then with a murmured curse he pulled back. 'Jeez, Imo. You are messing with my head.' He shoved his hands through his hair and nodded towards the centre of the restaurant. 'We're in public—in Richard Harvey's favourite restaurant. When Richard asks Marcel how we enjoyed our meal I'd like Marcel *not* to say we spent it in a clinch.'

Heat flushed her cheeks as she tried to quell the elation. She was messing with his head—who would have thought it? But...

'You're more than right. Here isn't the place. But—' She broke off as Marcel approached the table with a genial smile.

'Here we have a selection of dishes. The *amuse-*

bouches. Lemon, nuts, grapefruit and celery in a potato net. Haddock soufflé. And tuna in squid ink. Along with the best baguette in Paris.'

'It looks fabulous, Marcel. *Merci*.' Her words were spoken on automatic. Not even the scrumptious aroma that wafted up from the plate could distract her from the buzz her body radiated, the tingle of her lips where she'd brushed his cheek.

Once Marcel had gone, she met Joe's gaze.

'We have a problem,' he said. 'So I suggest we have a look round this apartment and then book separate rooms—preferably on separate floors—in a local hotel.'

'What about Richard? Staying there is part of his plan.'

'I'll come up with a reason if he asks. I doubt he will. The important thing will be the proposal. Whatever it is going on with us, I think distance is the key solution.'

'Or we give in to it.'

The words were blurted out without thought, spring-boarded to her brain from her instincts.

His body stilled and then he shook his head. 'No. Bad idea. We work together so that is not an option.'

'I get that—and, hell, I'd normally agree. But in this case the business is done. You've already made a decision about the proposal. And I swear to you I will give it my all. I am excited about the opportunity to do this for Langley. But I'm not propositioning you out of gratitude or because I want anything else.'

'So why *are* you propositioning me?'

'Because I've never felt like this before. And once, Joe—just once in my life—I want to succumb to lust. To say sod the rules. Not to be sensible. For one night.'

Hell, it wasn't too much to ask, was it? That for once she could ride the wave and not do the right thing? Sure, there was a part of her brain that was covering its eyes, unable to look, *shocked* by the sheer effrontery of this version of Imogen Lorrimer. But, damn it, she was going to ignore it.

'That's what you do, isn't it? One-night stands?'

'I thought they weren't your thing.' Joe picked his glass up and put it back down again, his eyes dark with desire.

Her lungs seemed to have forgotten how to function; breathing was problematic. 'I've changed my mind.'

A moment's pause during which his brown eyes bored into her expression. 'You're sure? One night? No strings? Because I can't offer anything else, Imogen.' He raised his hand before she could protest. 'I don't mean job-wise. I mean emotionally or time-wise. I don't tick your boxes.'

'One night is all I want as well, Joe. I'm not in the market for a relationship right now.' She needed time to regroup, update her tick-list. 'I've just come out of one. Plus—' She broke off. There was no need to explain to Joe that she didn't trust this whole insane attraction, that she would never risk letting it control her. That was the beauty of a one-night stand. 'I promise you this is all about the sex.'

A long moment and then he gusted out a sigh, his expression unreadable, before he smiled—the toe-curling, hair-frizzing version. 'Then let's eat and get out of here.'

How was she supposed to eat? Her appetite for food had legged it over the horizon long ago. All she wanted to savour right now was Joe; her nerves stretched taut with need.

But somehow she made it through the exquisite combination of tastes: the bite and tang of roast lobster flavoured with lemon and ginger, the intensity of a seafood bisque complemented by seaweed bread. But all the time she was oh-so aware of the solid thickness of Joe's thigh next to hers, the pressure of his knee under the table, the plane and angle of his strong jaw, the way the chandeliers glinted over the dark spikes of his hair.

The promise in his eyes made her tummy swirl in anticipation. Until finally—*finally*—they had eaten the last bite of a superbly light pistachio soufflé, had exchanged compliments with Marcel and could exit the restaurant.

Imogen welcomed the cool evening breeze on her face, though she couldn't help a small shiver as it hit her sensitised skin. Without speaking Joe shrugged off his jacket and placed it round her shoulders. Warmth encased her inside and out.

'Thank you.'

His hand clasped hers in a firm grip. 'No problem. The apartment isn't far.'

'Good. I'm…' *Burning. Yearning. Desperate.*

He looked down at her. 'Me too,' he said, with a sudden low chuckle that rippled into the breeze and tugged her lips into an answering smile.

Half-walking half-running, they wended their way along the pavement.

'It should be just down this alley,' he said, already digging in his pocket for the keys.

They reached a navy blue wooden door—he shoved the key into the lock and thrust the door open.

And came to an abrupt halt.

She could see why: the room they had stepped into was…*sumptuous*. Decadent. Luxurious. With warm red walls, rugs and throws that begged to be touched, deep crimson and gold curtains that would cocoon the room and its occupants against the outer world.

Then she saw the mural on the wall directly opposite the door.

A man and a woman entwined together, their naked bodies sinuous and beautiful. The pose intense, passionate, vivid.

Imogen swallowed, and then moistened her lips to relieve her parched mouth as her awareness of Joe further heightened. But with awareness came worry, and a sudden shyness tensed her body. What if she didn't come up to scratch? Surely this apartment was meant for women who were more...more beautiful, experienced, sexy?

Then Joe moved behind her, his body heat warming her as his fingers massaged her shoulders.

'You OK?' he murmured.

'My heart is beating so damn hard it's like I'm consumed—and yet I'm scared that I'll mess this up.'

Disappoint you.

'Not possible.'

His fingers continued to wreak their magic and she wriggled in sheer appreciation.

'But if you've changed your mind...'

A last lingering doubt snaked through her brain and she quashed it ruthlessly. This was her chance to experience something she might never experience again. Yes, lust was dangerous—but it was a danger she was fully aware of and had no intention of falling prey to.

As for the risk of disappointing Joe... Every molecule in her body told her that they'd work it out. This was *her* night and she'd regret it for ever if she didn't take it.

'No. I haven't changed my mind.'

'Good,' he growled as his hands slid to her shoulders, glissaded down to her waist.

He nuzzled her neck and at the touch of his lips she shivered, arched to give him better access. As she did so her gaze fell on the mural and she saw it in a new light— a picture of two normal people who were following their instincts, engaged in something natural and beautiful.

The realisation sent a thrill through her, and suddenly she needed to see Joe—see the man who was already giving her such pleasure.

As if he felt the same he stood back and turned her, so she was flush against the hard plane of his chest. The light scent of sandalwood mixed with sheer Joe assaulted her senses. Imogen looked up at him and her breath caught in her throat at the sight of the raw desire that dilated his pupils.

Standing on tiptoe, she looped her arms round his neck, buried her fingers in the thick brown hair. Joe's broad hands curved round her waist and his mouth covered hers. Imogen savoured the tang of pistachio and the flavour of mint leaf as his tongue swept the bow of her mouth and she parted her lips. Sensations rocketed through her as his tongue stroked hers, sliding and tangling and tormenting, and she matched him stroke for stroke.

She pushed against him, desperate to be closer, for more, pressing heavy breasts against his chest. His hands plunged down from her waist to cup her bottom, and she moaned into his mouth as momentum built and strummed inside her.

Breaking their kiss, he stepped backwards and sank down onto the deep crimson sofa, pulling her onto his lap, the strength of his thighs hard under hers.

Her clumsy-with-need fingers fumbled at the buttons of his shirt and tugged the silken black edges apart. Then *finally* she touched his skin, ran her hands over his packed chest.

Joe found the zip of her dress and tugged it down in one deft movement, gliding the gauzy material over her shoulders and down her arms, freeing her breasts.

'Jeez...' he breathed. 'You are gorgeous, Imogen.'

His large hands cupped her breasts and as he circled her standing-to-attention nipples. Imogen arched backwards in ecstasy. Then in one smooth movement he lifted her off his lap and laid her down on the expanse of the sofa.

'I need to see all of you,' he said roughly as his hands pulled her dress down.

Lifting her hips, she felt the material slide down and

off into a pool on the floor, followed by the lacy wisp of her knickers.

Joe's heated gaze glittered over her. 'So beautiful...' he murmured

Imogen allowed her gaze to run down his body, saw the impressive bulge that strained the zipper of his trousers. A quiver of anticipation thrilled through her.

'Joe?'

'Yes.'

'I think you need to take your clothes off. Things seem to be a little out of balance at the moment.'

'Your wish is my command, beautiful.'

In one lithe move he stood on the plush carpet and shucked off trousers and boxers to stand before her in glorious naked splendour.

Unfamiliar exultation shimmered over her that he could be so aroused by her body. Propping herself on her elbows, she let her gaze absorb every glorious millimetre of him—the light sheen of his sculpted torso, the ripped abs, the thick muscular thighs—and she shivered, imprinted the memory on her brain.

He smiled at her. 'Seen your fill?' he asked with a delectable quirk of his eyebrow.

'I could look at you for hours.'

It was nothing but the truth, and the knowledge that she'd love to draw him, to try and capture his arrogant male beauty on paper, crossed her mind. *No way, Imo.*

Instead, 'But I can think of other things to do right now.'

'As I said, your wish—'

'Then come here,' she said.

CHAPTER SEVEN

JOE PULLED THE fridge door open and welcomed the stream of cold air that hit him as he inspected the contents. As he'd suspected there was everything he needed for an impromptu midnight picnic—he wouldn't expect anything less from Lovers' Tryst. And he wanted Imogen to know that she deserved champagne and caviar and strawberries and cream, even if they weren't sensible.

Though the real reason he was here in the kitchen wasn't only food and drink—he needed a moment to regroup. The past hour had been sensational, and yet his body still hummed with desire. As if it was greedy to make the most of every hour of this night.

But he wanted this to be special for Imogen—more than just for the sex. Her words from the restaurant echoed in his ears. *'Because I've never felt like this before. And once, Joe—just once in my life—I want to succumb to lust. To say sod the rules. Not to be sensible. For one night.'* There had been wistfulness in her voice, along with the certainty of what she wanted—and it had called to something in him.

Convinced him to just once break a rule. There was no harm in it. Imogen had been right—he'd made the decision to let her run with the proposal and that decision had been made with no ulterior motive in mind. They were here for a night. From tomorrow morning it would be all about work, and soon he would leave Langley and move on. Rules Two and Three were still in place. 'One Night Only'. 'Never Look Back'.

The thought brought a certain relief as he loaded a tray and pushed the fridge door closed. He exited the kitchen and made his way down the corridor to the bedroom.

Breath whistled between his teeth as he took in the opulent splendour. An enormous circular bed with a curved wooden barred headboard dominated the floor and mirrors mastered the wall space.

Imogen sat cross-legged on the bed, dressed in a thick white towelling robe. 'It's a little unnerving to see myself from all angles,' she said. She gazed at the tray and her face lit up. 'I can't believe I'm saying this, but I'm ravenous.'

'It's all the exercise,' he said as he stepped forward and lowered the tray onto the bedside table. 'Champagne?'

'Yes, please.'

Minutes later they had plates balanced on their laps and a glass of bubbles in their hands.

'Thank you for this. It's incredible,' she said. 'I can safely say I've never eaten caviar in bed at midnight before. I've never eaten caviar at all.' The glance she swept at him was a touch shy. 'I thought one-night stands were just about the sex.'

Her words sent a small cold shock straight to his chest; when had he ever contemplated a midnight picnic before?

'No need for thanks. All I did was open the fridge.' *But you went looking*, a small voice pointed out. 'Seemed a shame to waste the contents.'

Imogen paused, a caviar-spread cracker halfway to her lips. 'Don't sweat it, Joe,' she said. 'I meant what I said. I don't want any more than a one-night stand. I'm just happy that it's turning out to be a definite once-in-a-lifetime experience.'

Since when had he been so readable? 'So you still don't believe in one-night stands?'

Her slim shoulders lifted in a small shrug. 'I can't see the point in them.'

'Really? Then I must have done something wrong.'

For a second she looked discomfited, her lips forming the cutest circle, and then she chuckled. 'You know damn well you did everything completely right. But it wouldn't feel right to do this on a regular basis. Like I said, I want a lot more than sex from a relationship and I won't risk getting blindsided by lust.'

'I thought we did pretty good on the lust front. Don't you agree?'

'Yes.' Her lips curved up in a sudden sweet smile. 'This has been totally amazing. But in a long-term relationship there are other things that are way more important.'

'Fair enough. But why not go for it all? Security, shared goals *and* great sex.'

Imogen blinked, as if the idea had never even occurred to her as a possibility, and then she shook her head and sipped her champagne. 'Honestly? I think a dynamite attraction would fuzz my brain and my perspective. I don't want physical desire to affect how I think and reason, or cause me to make stupid decisions. I've seen how that works out. My mother married my father because she fell in lust—and, believe me, their marriage is *everything* I don't want mine to be.'

The vehemence in her voice twanged a chord of empathy in him. 'Yet they've stayed together, haven't they?'

Perhaps Imogen knew the answer as to why two unsuited people stayed together despite every reason in the world to separate. An image of his own parents came to his mind and he felt the familiar gnarling of emotions in his gut. Frustration, confusion, anger, bewilderment.

Max and Karen McIntyre—good-looking, rich and devoted to each other. Or so they had appeared to Joe. Because he'd seen what he'd wanted to see or what they'd wanted him to see? Little wonder that he'd been sent to

boarding school—he could only imagine the strain the
pretence must have cost his parents.

'Yes,' Imogen said. 'They have. I think it's because in
some dreadful way they've become codependent. So used
to the shouting and the arguments and the bitterness they
can't imagine leaving. They've made a mess of it and I
don't want that—I certainly don't want that for my children. So I think I'll stick to my tick-list and keep sexual
attraction off it. It's not a big deal.'

Given her earlier responsiveness, her sheer uninhibited enjoyment, that was hard to believe. And anyway…
'Don't take this the wrong way, but clearly the tick-list
didn't work with Steve.'

'Noooo. But the principle is still sound. All I need to
do is amend the list to make sure I avoid men who are
still hung up on a previous girlfriend.' A small sigh escaped her lips. 'You'd think that would have been obvious, wouldn't you? Instead I was sure I could be the one
who'd help him get over her—be there for him, build up
a relationship. *Hah!*'

Joe frowned as he considered her words. 'You're telling me Steve left you for his ex?'

'Yup. It's even worse, in fact.' Her hands clenched round
a fold of red sheet.

'What happened?'

Jutting out her chin, she gazed at him almost defiantly,
her blue-grey eyes daring him to feel pity. 'I gave Steve
tickets for a cruise for his thirtieth birthday a few months
ago. He took Simone instead of me and proposed to her on
the cruise. They're getting married in a couple of months.'

'For real?'

'I don't think you could make that up.'

'Well, I'd like to say I'm sorry. But I'm not. The man
sounds like an absolute tosser and you're way better off
without him.'

Imogen's lips curved up in a sudden smile. 'So no sympathy?'

'Nope.' He topped up their glasses and raised his. 'I think it's more a cause for celebration. To a new start.'

The chime as crystal hit crystal was oddly significant, and as if feeling it Imogen wriggled backwards to lean against the graceful curve of the headboard.

Shaking away the emotion, Joe took her empty plate from her. 'You done?'

'Yes.'

'Good. Because I have some excellent ideas for what to do with the strawberries and cream.'

She moistened her lips. 'Care to share?'

'Oh, yes. I have every intention of sharing. Now, come here. And drop the sheet.'

Batting her eyelashes at him in an exaggerated fashion, she pushed the sheet down in one fluid movement. 'Your wish is my command,' she murmured, and the hot rush of desire swept away all other thoughts.

Imogen opened her eyes and for a heartbeat confusion fuzzed her brain—until the twinge of hitherto unused muscles brought back a flood of glorious memories. Memories that culminated in finally falling asleep wrapped in Joe's arms, her cheek nestled against the smattering of hair on his chest.

Rolling over, she realised her only bedmate now was the finger of light that filtered through the slats of the blinds to hit the rumpled, cold red sheet.

A sense of bereavement socked her, and Imogen gritted her teeth. *No!* The night was over and waking up naked in bed together was not the way forward for the professional day ahead. Joe at least had had the sense to realise it.

Yet how could she erase those memories that still buzzed through her veins and exhilarated her body. Surely she wouldn't be human if she didn't regret the bone-deep knowledge that she'd never plumb the depths of lust as deeply again? For the first time ever she truly understood exactly how her parents might have got carried away by a tornado of passion. How they might have believed that if their bodies were so in tune so must their minds be.

Well, Imogen knew differently, but it was probably just as well not to put that knowledge to any further test.

So…no regrets. Instead it was time to haul herself out of bed and start to concentrate on work.

Entering the bathroom, she did her very best to look at it with the eye of an interior designer.

But how could she when her skin tingled as it relived the memory of leaning back against those glittering mirrored tiles, water jetting down, Joe soaping her, his muscles under her fingers smooth, hard, delectable as she returned the favour. The memory made her dizzy her and she clenched her hands around the cool edge of the sink.

Come on.

Lists. That was the way forward. As she showered she focused on the minutiae of the bathroom. Mirrored tiles, wet room, scented candles, exotic shampoos…

Shower over, she tugged her hair into a ponytail, pulled on the simple jeans and striped T-shirt she'd purchased the day before and pushed the bedroom door open.

This was fifty shades of awkward—and her nerves tautened as she approached the kitchen. The aroma of strong coffee tickled her nostrils as she entered and walked across the marble floor to the open French doors.

She put one hand to the side of the door for balance as she took in the scene.

Joe sat at a circular wrought-iron table—damp from the shower, hair spiked up, jeans and navy T sculpting the toned strength of a body she knew by heart. There was a cup of coffee in front of him, his laptop was up and running, his phone was to his ear. So gorgeous… The temptation to grab him by the hand and drag him back to the bedroom had her tightening her grip on the doorjamb.

Moving on. Maybe she should concentrate on the exotic plants that hid the patio from the street, on the hum of traffic, the sunlight striping the verdant leaves. Anything but Joe.

He nodded as he spoke. 'May the best man win. I'll see you on Wednesday.'

He dropped the phone onto the table and suddenly Imogen knew she couldn't face him just yet.

Coffee. The world would come into focus with the help of caffeine.

Hurriedly she turned and headed towards the coffee machine. She just needed a minute to regroup—*breathe in, breathe out and repeat*—then, coffee cup in hand, she headed outside to join him.

Joe was intent on his laptop, his conversation over, a frown creasing his forehead.

'Morning,' Imogen said, and foreboding weighted her stomach. Joe looked formidable—a far cry from the man she'd had a midnight picnic with in bed.

'Good morning.'

Fighting the urge to turn and run, Imogen forced her unwilling legs forward, pulled out a chair and sat down.

What now? For the first time since they had entered the apartment Imogen wondered if she had screwed up monumentally by sleeping with Joe. 'Um…'

His gaze was unreadable, his expression unyielding as he looked across the table at her, and Imogen felt the heat of embarrassment curdle her insides. This was not the expression she'd wanted to see.

Come on, Imo. What did you expect? The night was over and Joe was back in ruthless businessman mode—there was no reason for him to look at her with warmth.

Yet surely what they had shared last night had to mean *something*?

'So how does this work?' she blurted out. 'This is uncharted territory for me. I don't know the etiquette of the morning after. What usually happens?'

'Breakfast and goodbye.' He picked up his coffee cup. 'Unfortunately not an option in this case.'

'Unfortunately?' Hurt crashed into anger and created fury.

For a second she thought she saw emotion flash across his face, and then the guard was back up, his jaw set, the outline of his mouth grim.

'Come on, Imogen, let's be grown-up about this. I could write a whole tick-list of my own with reasons why last night should not have happened.' He closed his eyes and grimaced. 'I can't believe I said that. I meant a list—not a tick-list.'

Imogen forced herself not to flinch. She'd shared something important with him last night about her parents' disastrous marriage and her need for a tick-list, and now he was mocking her.

'I'd rather have a tick-list than some sort of cold, emotionless relationship avoidance criteria.'

A sigh gusted through the air as he pushed his chair back over the paved stones. 'And this is exactly why last night was a mistake. We need to work together—not sit here trading *emotional* insults.'

Imogen opened her mouth and then closed it again, focusing on the backdrop—the terracotta pots and the mosaic patterns of the outdoor tiles

Joe was right. This was about Langley. About keeping Langley safe from Ivan Moreton by winning the Richard Harvey project.

Imogen frowned as Joe's earlier words echoed in her ears. *'May the best man win. See you on Wednesday.'*

'Who were you on the phone to earlier?'

His fingers drummed a tattoo on the table. 'Ivan More-ton.'

'You're going to see Ivan Moreton on Wednesday?'

'Yes.'

'But…'

'But what?'

There was no quarter in his voice or expression; any minute now she'd see icicles form as he spoke.

'Did you think last night would affect my buy-out decision?'

'No!'

What *had* she thought? She'd foolishly, erroneously, stupidly thought the man she'd shared a bed and so much more with last night wasn't capable of selling off the company to a douchebag like Ivan Moreton.

Cold realisation touched her with icy fingers—she'd done the thing she'd sworn she wouldn't. Let lust—the way Joe had made her *body* feel—affect her judgement. Joe had never claimed to be Mr Nice Guy—Imogen had repainted him to suit herself. Just because he could make her body achieve the heights of ecstasy, she'd rewritten his personality.

Idiot. Idiot. Idiot.

Shame coated her very soul when she remembered how she'd spilled her guts about tick-lists, her parents' marriage, Steve and Simone. And what had he shared in return? Zilch—a great big zip-a-dee-doo-dah zero. Humiliation jumped into the mix. Maybe he hadn't even been listening—maybe all his women experienced the urge to confide in him post-orgasm and he just tuned them out until he was ready for the next round.

'Well?' he rasped.

'I have no expectations of you whatsoever.' Hauling in breath, she dug deep, located her pride and slammed her shoulders back. 'There is no need to worry that last night will make any difference at all to us working together.'

She'd made a monumental error and slept with the enemy—forgotten her work obligations and where her loyalty lay. It was time to make up for that. So she'd use what he'd given her—channel the fizz and the buzz, take the memories and turn them into creative vibes.

'*I* care about Langley and I will create a kick-ass proposal that will beat Graham's hands-down. And, yes, I do hope that influences your decision about selling out to Ivan Sleazeball Moreton.'

His email pinged and he glanced down at the laptop screen. For a second Imogen saw irritation cross his face.

'Trouble?' she asked. As long as it wasn't anything to do with Langley she damn well hoped that it was.

'Nothing I can't deal with.' He lifted his gaze. 'So, any ideas yet?'

'Give me a ch—' Just like that an idea shimmered into her brain, frothed and bubbled. 'Actually, yes, I do.'

He gestured with his hand. 'Go ahead. I'm listening.'

Imogen hesitated—right now she didn't even want to share air space with the guy, let alone tell him her idea. But, as she had so spectacularly forgotten last night, Joe McIntyre was the boss.

'I need to show Richard and Crystal that Langley can create an apartment that is essentially French—a place that combines fantasy and reality, a place where they can feel at home and on holiday all at the same time. A home with a sexy edge, with glitz and glamour, but somewhere to feel comfortable. For example—look at this kitchen. It's very minimalist…not really the sort of kitchen you could imagine cooking in. So I'd design a kitchen that conveys the chicness of croissants and coffee, the sexiness of caviar and champagne, but also the hominess of cooking a romantic boeuf bourgignon together. Then on the proposal I'd sketch all those elements.'

To her own irritation she realised she was holding her breath, waiting for Joe's opinion. *Please just let it be a need for the professional go-ahead. Nothing more.*

His fingers tapped on the wrought-iron of the tabletop as he thought.

'Sounds good. Come up with an idea like that for each room and I'll come up with a cost mock-up. Let's get to work.'

CHAPTER EIGHT

'DONE.' IMOGEN DROPPED the charcoal pencil onto the sheened mahogany Langley boardroom table and blew out a sigh. Exhaustion made her eyelids visibly heavy, and dark lashes swept down in a long blink as she reached for her cup of coffee. 'Here.' She pushed the piece of paper towards him. 'If you hate it don't tell me.'

Joe shook his head. 'I haven't hated anything yet.'

Far from it—over the past two days Imogen had produced some truly exceptional sketches. Perplexity made him frown yet again at her genuine inability to see her own talent. Instead doubt often clouded her vision and caused her to chew her lip in a way it was nigh on impossible not to be distracted by.

Not that he had given even the whisper of a hint of said distraction. After the sheer stupidity of his behaviour in Paris he'd made sure to keep to strictly professional boundaries. As for Imogen—once she'd got immersed in the project it had been as if she'd entered a world of her own.

'I know you haven't. But I'm worried neither of us can see straight any more—we're too knackered.'

She had a point; they'd worked round the clock. They'd worked in the apartment, worked on the Eurostar and come straight to Langley, where they'd set up shop. Grabbing only a few hours' shut-eye on the boardroom sofa.

'And,' she continued, 'this last room is pretty crucial—the master bedroom is meant to be the *pièce de résistance*.'

Full marks to her, he thought. Although a flush tinged

the angle of her cheeks, her voice and gaze were steady. Yet he knew she must be remembering their own bedroom interlude. He glanced down at the sketch and his heart thudded as images filtered across his brain. Imogen had taken the bedroom at Lovers' Tryst and delivered to it her own unique twist. No longer circular, the bed seemed suspended in the air.

'It's a floating bed,' she said. 'It's different and romantic. I know it may be more expensive, but…'

'I'll check.'

'No!' Her face paled as she nodded at the clock. 'Look at the time.'

'It's eleven.'

'Eleven *p.m.*'

'Oh, hell.' The impact of her words hit Joe with a sucker punch. 'Richard said first thing Monday morning and it's an hour until midnight. Do you think we need to get this over there now, rather than at nine a.m.?'

'I think Richard is quite capable of disqualifying us if we don't meet the exact letter of his instructions.'

'So we'd better get it couriered across right now. I'm on it. You get it packaged. We'll email it across as well.'

Anger spiked inside him, along with a surge of adrenalin—he should have spotted that midnight trap right from the get-go. Instead of pondering over Imogen's lack of self belief. Instead of interspersing working flat-out with his fight to sever the bonds of attraction that had him so distracted.

Imogen nodded and raced across the boardroom, and he pulled his phone out of pocket—this proposal would get to Richard Harvey on time if it killed him. No way would he let Langley down—that would *not* be acceptable. If he didn't know a courier service would get it there more quickly he'd take it himself.

Fifteen minutes later Imogen stared at him, worry painting creases on her forehead. 'It *will* get there, won't it?'

'Yes. I've used Mark before—he whizzes round London faster than the speed of light. And Richard's offices aren't that far away. Plus, we know the email made it. So we're covered.' He nodded. 'Well spotted, Imogen.'

'I should have thought of it before,' she said. 'But now I'm worried we've sent a proposal that's not as good as it could be. I thought we had a few more hours to polish it.'

'Don't be so hard on yourself. I didn't think of it at all.'

'You don't know Richard as well as I do.' She paced the room, long jean-clad legs striding the length of the boardroom table. 'I *want* this contract.'

Her smile was tremulous, and for an insane moment he wanted to pull her into a hug, slide his hand down her back and utter soothing words. Shock rooted him to the deep-pile carpet that covered the boardroom floor and he tried to school his features into professional support mode.

'So do I. I promise you it's a damn fine proposal and it's got a really good chance. You couldn't have done more than you did.'

'Huh. That's what I used to tell myself after exams. *You've worked really hard, Imogen, maybe this time you haven't messed it up.*' Her hand covered the slight curve of her tummy. 'Ugh. It makes me feel queasy.' Pressing her lips together, as if to stop the flow of further information, she resumed pacing.

Her words triggered a memory of Imogen in his office just a week before, telling him about her ten-year-old self bringing a report home and her mother's disappointment. He recalled her words in the Michelin-starred restaurant, her fear of undertaking the proposal, and a pang of understanding hit him.

Instinct prompted the words he had used so many times with his sisters. 'You have given this your all and no one can ask more than that. Including yourself. If we don't win this proposal you haven't let anyone down.'

'That's easy for you to say,' she said, coming to a stop in front of him 'If I lose and Graham wins there's a bigger chance you'll sell Langley to Ivan. For you that's just business—another day on the job. But for me... I will have let Peter and Harry down. They will be devastated, and in their state of health that will have a knock-on effect. And I will always wonder if I should have called Belinda in.'

He shifted backwards slightly—not a good plan to have the lush curve of her breasts in his line of sight. 'That was my call, and no matter what happens I stand by that decision. You are taking too much on yourself. Both Peter and Harry have seen this proposal and they love it.'

'That doesn't guarantee I'll win. And if I don't, Langley is one step further to ending up in Ivan's hands. That's a fact, isn't it?'

To his own surprise Joe felt a prod of guilt, even as he forced his features to remain neutral. No way could he let emotional reasoning affect a business decision.

'Yes.'

'There you go, then. *My* responsibility. My bad if it goes wrong.' Her hair shielded her expression as she continued her relentless striding across the room.

He rose and strode towards her, blocked her path as she paced. 'Stop.'

This was important enough that he would force himself to ignore the way her delicate scent enveloped him, would allow himself to get close to her.

'It will *not* be your fault if Langley ends up in a buy-out situation. You will *not* have let Peter down—or Langley. Promise me you get that.'

Her chest rose and fell, her blue-grey eyes were wide as she stared up at him, and suddenly he felt all kinds of a fool. What was he doing, overreacting like this? If only she wasn't so beautiful—ink-stains, smudged eyes, creased T-shirt and all.

Stepping backwards, out of temptation's way, he forced himself to sound casual. '*I* will be making the decisions as to Langley's future—no matter what happens you can absolve yourself from blame. In fact I'll provide you with a life-size photograph of me and a set of darts. How's that?'

'It sounds like a plan.'

A thoughtful frown creased her brow—almost as if she were trying to figure something out. *Join the club.*

'Joe?'

'Yes?'

'I'll still be throwing those darts, and I'm still a bit of a wreck, but…you've made me feel better. Thank you.'

'No problem.' Embarrassment still threatened and he shrugged it off. 'In the meantime, if you want to head home now I'll call you a taxi.'

Imogen shook her head. 'I don't think I'll be able to sleep—I'm too wired on coffee and adrenalin. And what if Richard gets back to us now? I'll stay here—but you don't have to stay as well.'

As if he'd leave her in a deserted building at this time of night. Hell, call him old-fashioned, but he wouldn't leave *any* woman in that situation. Anyway…

'I want to hear Richard's decision too.'

It was no more than the truth—he did want Langley to win this bid as a stepping stone on its way to recovery. And he did also want to be with Imogen when the verdict arrived—to see her lips curve into her gorgeous smile if they won or to offer comfort if they hadn't. That was fair enough. They'd worked incredibly hard for this proposal—had bonded *professionally*.

'Why don't you order a pizza? I don't think we remembered to eat today.'

'Sounds like a great idea,' she said.

His tablet pinged to indicate the arrival of an email. He glanced down and supressed a groan. Leila again. This was now officially out of hand and he had no idea what to do about it.

'Your mystery caller again?' Imogen asked. 'The one who makes you sigh every time you get an email?'

Nearly choking in an attempt to inhale a puff of air, he shook his head. 'She's *not* a mystery caller.'

For a nanosecond Imogen's shoulders tensed, and then she turned the movement into a shrug. 'If she isn't mysterious why don't you tell me who she is?' She hesitated. 'It may help to talk about it.'

'No.'

He regretted the curtness of the syllable as soon as it dropped from his lips, but the thought of explaining the Leila situation in full had moisture sheening the back of his neck.

With an expressive upturn of her palms she rolled her eyes. 'Fair enough. It was just a thought. I'll go and order the pizza.'

Joe watched her as she picked up the phone and then dropped his gaze to the email. Incredulity descended, causing him to reread the words in the hope that he'd got it wrong. *Now what?*

His gut informed him that he was seriously mishandling Leila, his actions being dictated by the sear of guilt. His eyes veered up to Imogen—could it be time to acknowledge that he needed some help, here? Every bone in his body revolted at the idea, but as he read the email again panic roiled in his stomach.

There was no choice—he couldn't afford to mess this up and, like it or not, he was way out of his depth.

Imogen placed the order, trying and failing not to watch Joe. It didn't look as if the email was giving him joy. In fact she was pretty sure he'd groaned—and she didn't think it was because she'd ordered him an extra-hot pepperoni, double on the chillies.

His mystery woman was none of her business. Joe had made that more than clear and he was right. It was personal stuff, and she and Joe had already got *plenty* up close and personal. Heaven knew what impulse had even made her offer to help—perhaps it had been the way he had clearly wanted to help *her*?

Tucking her phone back into her jeans pocket, she marched over to him, pulled out the seat opposite and plonked herself down. 'Pizza won't be long.'

'Great.' Thrusting his hand through his already spiky hair, he inhaled audibly. 'Um...now I've read the email, if you're still up for that offer of help, I could do with a little feminine insight.'

Surprise made her raise her eyebrows; it must be bad, because it was clear from the way he had squeezed out each word that the request had been made with total reluctance.

'You *are* a little pale about the gills.'

'I'm feeling a little pale about the everywhere.'

Imogen flicked a glance at Joe's screen and curiosity bubbled to the surface. 'OK, then. Tell me how you can use a female point of view and I'll give it a shot.'

Joe gestured at the email. 'The mystery woman is Leila. She's an ex-girlfriend from seven years ago. I hadn't heard from her since the split, then three weeks ago she emailed me an invitation to her wedding. Which is less than two weeks from now. You may have read about it—her fiancé is Howard Kreel.'

Imogen blinked. 'Your ex-girlfriend is Leila Went-worth? The woman who is engaged to the son of one of the planet's richest men?'

She and Mel and most of the country had discussed the wedding, marvelling over Leila's blonde beauty and the entire rags-to-riches Cinderella story, with an element of superhero thrown in. Howard had rescued Leila in an alleyway, where she had been on the verge of being robbed, and their relationship had grown and flourished from there—to the point where now they were planning a three-day wedding extravaganza in the Algarve.

'Wow.'

'Yeah, *wow*.' The sarcastic inflexion was accompanied by a lip-curl.

Obviously Joe was less than entranced by the prospect. In which case...

'It is kind of weird that she has asked you, but maybe she has literally invited everyone she has ever known. If you don't feel comfortable my advice is not to go.'

Difficult to believe he hadn't worked that out for himself.

Joe shook his head. A faint colour touched his cheekbones and a shadow fleeted across his eyes. 'There's more to it than that. It's...' He drummed his fingers on the table. 'I need to go.'

'Why?'

'It doesn't matter why.'

'Even though you don't want to?'

Impossible to believe that Joe would attend any function he didn't want to. Confusion along with a hint of foreboding threaded through her tummy.

'I don't have a problem going. The problem is that Leila has started sending me emails on a daily basis.'

'Saying what?'

Joe expelled a sigh, and for a moment he looked so bewildered she felt an irrational misplaced urge to lean over and smooth the creases from his forehead.

'Saying how important love is and how I must learn to embrace it—how important it is to find the person of your dreams. Pages and pages of it.'

'So how have you replied?'

'I tell her that my life is very happy as it is, but thanks for the advice. But the emails keep on coming.'

The woman sounded unhinged—which begged the question: why was Joe going along with her?

'I'm not getting this. What happened to being ruthless? Tell her to get knotted and say that you have your love-life perfectly under control.'

'I can't do that.' Joe shifted in his seat, discomfort clear in the set of his jaw and in the frown that slashed his forehead. 'This is important to her—I just need to figure out why.'

Realisation dawned with a sense of inevitability that stuck in her craw. Joe was hung up on an ex-girlfriend. What was it about her that attracted men who held ten-foot torches for old lovers?

'You OK?' Joe asked.

'I'm fine.'

What else could she say? All she'd wanted from Joe was a great night between the sheets. He'd given her that—it made no difference if he'd harboured feelings for an ex whilst he did so. Yet somehow… Damn it, it did. Bad enough that he regretted the night—now the attraction was even further sullied. But that wasn't Joe's problem. It was hers. She'd offered her insight and she'd make good on that.

'Absolutely fine. What did today's email say? Obviously she's upped the ante or you wouldn't need my input.'

'Today's email informs me that Leila has lined me up with a series of potential girlfriends because she wants me to—' he hooked his fingers in the air to indicate quote marks '—"find true love and embrace the peace and inner tranquillity that this true love will bring".' He snorted and pushed away from the table. 'Little wonder I'm a bit green about the gills.'

Imogen frowned—why on earth would Leila want to

set Joe up with a friend of hers? Come to that, why was she so worried about Joe's love life?

Joe exhaled a sigh. 'No way do I want to face a line-up of women, all trying to bring me to a sense of inner tranquillity. Come to that, it would hardly be fair to them. I'm not on the looking-for-love market.'

'Just don't go. That way the line-up can't get you.'

'It's not that's simple, Imogen.' He tipped his palms in the air. 'If Steve and Simone ask you to their wedding will you go?'

'That's different.'

'Why?'

'For a start my mum and Steve's mum are friends—or at least they went to school together. So no doubt my parents will go, and Mum will want me to go so that everyone can see that I'm OK. And Steve and I were together only recently—we share lots of mutual friends and I guess I'll want to show them that I'm not licking my wounds somewhere. So it's a matter of parental pressure and pride. That's not the case for you.'

'But it is important to you that everyone thinks you're OK?'

'Well, yes…'

'It's important to me to see that Leila is OK. And I need her to believe that *I* am OK.'

The words shouldn't hurt as much as they did—yet each one impacted her chest with meaning. Joe was still in love with Leila, but he was willing to stand aside and watch her go to her true love. Leila knew Joe still loved her and was doing her best to get him to move on. Any minute now Imogen would need a bucket.

'If it's important to Leila that you find love then I guess you'd better find a woman, fall in love and take her to the wedding.'

Then perhaps as a finale everyone could watch a herd of flying pigs perform a musical.

'Don't be sil—'

Joe broke off, leant back in the stylish boardroom chair, and surveyed her with a thoughtful expression that set alarm bells off in her mind. The last thing she wanted was for Joe to suspect her state of mind—hell, she wasn't sure she understood it herself yet. She just knew she was sick and tired of hearing about men and their love for their exes. Been there. Done that. And it was getting old.

To her relief the intercom buzzed to herald the arrival of the pizza.

Joe lifted a hand. 'Just give me a second. I'll grab the pizzas.'

'OK.'

Imogen had no intention of taking this conversation further. Joe would have to figure this one out on his own. Maybe he should storm the wedding and declare his love. After all, surely he wasn't the sort of man to stand aside and let the love of his life marry someone else without a fight.

It was nothing to do with her. Yet the insidious feeling of *yuck* still made her skin clammy. It seemed every which way she was doomed to being second-best.

CHAPTER NINE

JOE HANDED SOME money over to the pizza delivery boy and balanced the boxes on both hands as he strode back to the boardroom, his brain whirring as he analysed his idea from all angles.

He pushed the door open and glanced round. Imogen sat at her laptop, intent on the screen, her hair hiding her expression from him, body tilted away from the door.

'Pizza's up.' Joe walked to the other end of the boardroom, put the boxes on the table and lifted the lids.

Twisting away from the screen, she narrowed her eyes and stared at the pizza.

Joe frowned. 'Has Richard called? Is something wrong?'

There must be some reason for her obvious withdrawal.

'Nope and nope.'

'Come on, Imo.' Two sisters had taught him exactly when *nope* meant *Yes—I'm really pissed off.*

'I'm fine.'

'Great. Then would it be OK if we keep talking?'

Pulling out a slice of pizza, he took a bite.

'Mmm…'

She gave a roll of her eyes and an exasperated sigh that blew her fringe upwards…but she rose from her seat and headed over with the instinctive grace that he loved to watch.

She picked up the box. 'There's nothing to talk about. You asked for my advice. I gave it. You won't listen to it. Topic closed.'

'I've got a proposition for you.'

'For *me*?' Eyebrows raised, she halted in mid turn away from the table.

'Yup. You come to Leila's wedding with me and I'll come to Steve's wedding with you.' He allowed his lips to quirk upwards in his most persuasive smile.

'That's a joke, right?'

'Nope.' He tilted his palms upward. 'It's the perfect solution.'

'I wasn't aware *I* had a problem.'

'Think about it, Imogen. You said you wanted to go to Steve's wedding and show everyone you're over him. What better way than to take a man with you? You can present me however you like. As a man you're enjoying a wild, uninhibited affair with or as a boyfriend—either way, it should give everyone the message that you're over him.'

'I may have a bona fide date of my own by then. Either a sex god or the perfect man.'

'Maybe you will.' The idea was not one he wanted to contemplate or encourage. 'But most likely you won't.'

Her eyes narrowed. 'Why's that?'

'Because it's going to take you at least a year to find a man who ticks all the boxes on your list. That or a miracle.'

'Really?' Her voice would have created ice in a desert.

'Anyway, the point is you can help me and I can help you. You come to Leila's wedding and you'll be showing people you're *already* over Steve. In style.'

For a second he thought he had her, and then she shook her head and redirected that laser look at him.

'So I can help you *how*, exactly?'

'It's simple. I take you, we pretend to be in love—that will make Leila believe I'm OK and I'll be safe from the line-up of women.'

It was genius. As long as he ignored the small voice

that pointed out that it would mean spending three days *and nights* with Imogen Lorrimer.

Not a problem. After all, they had already had one night together—he'd already broken Rule One. It was inconceivable that he would break Rule Two. Even if Imogen wanted to—and he was damn sure she didn't.

'So I'll be camouflage?'

There was an edge to her voice that indicated Imogen was failing to see the mastermind qualities of the idea. But he really couldn't see her issue. It had been her suggestion that had sparked the idea in the first place.

'Yes.'

She slammed the pizza box down on the table with a thunk. 'Can you not see how insulting that is?'

'Insulting to whom?'

'Me!'

Joe stared at her; her blue-grey eyes sparkled with anger and her hands were clenched into small fists. 'How do you figure that?'

'You really can't see it, can you? I stupidly told you about Steve and Simone, but you still don't get it.'

'So why don't you calm down and explain it?'

'Fine. You—' a slender finger was jabbed towards his chest '—still love Leila. You don't want Leila to know you're holding a torch the size of the Empire State Building for her but, believe you me, it's obvious—and she knows it. If I come with you everyone will watch you mooning over Leila and feel sorry for me for being second-best. Or however far down the list I come in your table of one-night stands. So, thanks—but no thanks. I am *not* coming along to be an object of pity.'

Anger that Imogen would believe he was such an insensitive jerk clawed at his chest. 'That is the most stupid analysis of the situation imaginable.'

'*Hah!* Face the truth. You are nothing more than an insensitive arrogant bastard with his head up his bum. Well, you can find some other sucker. Hell, seems like I've been second-best or not up to scratch all my life. I'm not doing it again. No freaking way!'

His vocal cords appeared to have stopped working in the face of her torrent of words. Before he could find so much as a syllable her phone buzzed.

Tugging it out of her pocket, she looked down at the screen and the angry flush leeched from her skin. 'It's Richard.'

Joe raked a hand over his face and attempted to locate his professional business head. 'Pick it up. And put him on loudspeaker.'

Imogen hauled in an audible breath, pressed a button and lifted the phone. She wrapped one arm around her stomach and said, 'Hi, Richard. Imogen speaking.'

Looking down, Joe realised his knuckles had whitened as he grasped the table edge—he couldn't remember the last time a business deal had mattered this much to him.

Imogen rocked to and fro on the balls of her feet, her face scrunched into creases of worry, and Joe felt his anger dissipate—to be replaced by a deep, almost painful hope that they'd won this proposal.

'I'm grand.' Richard's voice boomed. 'Thank you for your proposal. Crystal and I have discussed it, and Graham's, and…'

Joe watched as Imogen caught her lower lip in her teeth, felt his gut lurch in sympathy.

'Yours came in more expensive…'

Her shoulders slumped and Joe rose to his feet, striding around the table to take the phone, see if he could negotiate.

'But we absolutely loved the premise so we've decided to go with you.'

'*Yes!*'

He could feel the grin take over his face as he heard the words, saw the smile that illuminated Imogen's features as the conversation continued.

'Th...thank you so much, Richard. Absolutely. Yes. I'll get a contract across to you as soon as the office opens for business.'

Dropping the phone onto the table, she fist-pumped the air before doing a twirl—he could almost see the elation fizzing off her and it made his chest warm.

'Congratulations. You did good.'

'*We* did good. They loved it. I mean *really* loved it. You heard Richard—he said the idea was inspirational and that the sketches made him feel like he was living and breathing France. He also said that the proposal was balanced by a sensible and realistic budget that showed him we'd done our homework. *We* gave better value for money *and* showed a much better understanding of what they wanted.'

Another twirl and she ended up right next to him, so close that her delicate flowery scent assailed him. So close all he had to do was reach out and...

Her eyes widened as she looked up at him—and then she jumped backwards, shaking her head.

'I...I...need to let Peter and Harry know, and—'

'It's one a.m., Imogen. Best to wait until morning.'

'Of course... Um...well, thank you, Joe. I truly mean that.'

One long blink and then she smoothed her hands down her jeans, the rise and fall of her chest distracting him as she breathed deeply. Once, twice, thrice.

'Sorry I got a bit heated earlier. I hope that you work it out with Leila and the wedding goes all right.'

'Whoa. Not so fast.'

'What do you mean?'

'I mean we hadn't finished our conversation. I thought you'd just hit your groove, in fact.'

'Yes, well… Probably a good thing we were interrupted. Before I screeched along in my groove and got myself fired.'

Affront panged inside him. 'I wouldn't fire you because of a personal argument.'

Her nose wrinkled in obvious disbelief. 'Um…good to know. But as far as I am concerned the topic is over.'

'Think again. I am *not* still in love with Leila.' The idea was laughable, even if he didn't feel like cracking so much as a smile. 'You will *not* be seen as second-best.'

Imogen huffed out a sigh. 'It's not going to fly, Joe. You're kidding yourself if you truly believe you're not carrying a flaming torch for her. There is no other explanation. No girlfriend since Leila. Just one-night stands. An aversion to relationships. Going to her wedding to make her happy. Wanting her to believe you're OK. Willing to lie and undergo an elaborate charade rather than say no to her.'

For a second, shock had him bereft of speech—he could see exactly why Imogen had added up two and two and got approximately a million. But now what? It wouldn't be easy to convince her of her utter miscalculation without telling her a lot more than he wanted to share.

Joe drummed his fingers on his thigh as he weighed up just how badly he needed Imogen's cooperation. Damn it—he couldn't come up with a better solution to the whole Leila issue than to take Imogen to the wedding.

Bottom line: he needed her on board.

Though it was more than that—truth be told, he didn't want to feature in Imogen's brain as a man hung up on his ex. The idea of being lumped together with a git like Steve left an acrid tang. If he wanted to bring utter honesty to the table he could see that Imogen was hurt, and that made his skin prickle in discomfort.

So he would have to tell her the truth.

'I'm not holding a torch for Leila. Truth is, I owe her.'

'Owe her what?' Imogen's brow creased.

Guilt panged inside him at his past behaviour; discomfort gnawed his chest at the thought of the man he had been. *Come on, McIntyre. No truth…no lifeline at the wedding from hell.*

'Leila and I met nine years ago at uni.' A lifetime ago. 'We started going out.'

The cool surfing dude and the hot surfer chick. Tension shot down his spine.

'Then two years later my parents died in a car crash.'

Imogen stilled, her eyes widening in shock as she stretched her hand across the table. He let it lie. He needed to focus on getting the facts out—there was no need for sympathy along the way.

'Joe. I am so sorry. I had no idea. I can't even imagine what that must have been like. But it must have been devastating for you. For you all. Your sisters…'

'It was a difficult time.' Not that he had any intention of going into detail; the lid was not coming off *that* buried box of emotions. 'For me, for the twins, and for Leila as well.'

Imogen frowned. 'Difficult for Leila how?'

'I made it difficult. I had to grow up fast and I put pressure on her to do the same.'

'The twins?'

'Yes. It got complicated. Holly and Tammy were eleven; I was twenty-one.' Twenty-one with a promising surfing career ahead—not exactly parent-equivalent material. 'There were no relatives on the scene so Social Services intervened, questioned whether I could look after them or whether they would be better off in care.' The taste of remembered fear that his sisters would be wrested from him coated his throat. 'Obviously there was no way I could let them go but…that was tough for Leila to understand.'

Imogen scrunched up her nose in clear disapproval. 'So Leila jumped ship?'

'Yes. No discredit to her. She was twenty-one as well—she didn't want to settle down and raise two grieving, rebellious pre-teens who didn't even like her.'

Her shoulders hitched in a shrug. 'Hmm… Call me dim, but I don't get how that makes you owe her?'

'Because I didn't take her ship-jumping very well. I was desperate for us to stay together.'

He'd been a mess of confusion, frustration, fear and anger as he'd watched the life he'd thought he had unravel—as he'd realised everything he'd believed his parents to be had been an illusion. The idea that everything he'd thought he and Leila had was another fantasy had been hard to get a handle on.

'I thought love should conquer all and a woman should stand by her man. I believed that being in a stable relationship would help me in my case for winning custody of the twins.'

Her blue-grey eyes held an understanding he didn't merit.

'That seems more than reasonable, Joe. You must have been terrified and grieving and shocked. You needed your girlfriend's support.'

'Unfortunately I wasn't exactly firing on all cylinders, so I wasn't at home to reason. First I proposed marriage.' He gave a small mirthless laugh as he remembered his frenzied planning and his clumsy stupidity. The candlelit dinner, the violins, the ring bought with scraped-together money he'd ill been able to afford. 'Leila refused to marry me and I… Well, I reacted badly.'

Imogen rose and walked round the table to sit beside him, placed a warm hand over his and held on when he tried to pull away.

'Save your sympathy. Believe me, I don't deserve it. I

made Leila's life hell. I couldn't let it go. I begged, threatened, hounded her. I tried character assassination tactics and I made wild promises. The works.' Shame seared his gut, along with the bitter memory of his abject neediness. 'In the end she threatened me with a restraining order and I forced myself to back off before the custody case went down the pan. So, you see, I do owe her.'

Imogen's hand tightened over his. 'You're being pretty hard on yourself. You were in a bad place then, coping with a lot of emotions.'

'That didn't give me the right to stuff up someone else's life.'

'That's plain dramatic.'

'I wish. Leila has invited me to her wedding because her therapist has recommended it so she can have closure and truly move on in life with her husband. Turns out she's been racked with guilt all these years and it's prevented her from forming relationships. Even now she's had to work extremely hard in therapy to believe herself worthy of love.'

'Joe, this all sounds a bit screwy to me. Wouldn't it be more sensible for the two of you to meet up in private, not at her wedding? Talk it through?'

He rubbed the back of his neck. 'Apparently her wedding is symbolic for both of us. She's the injured party here—I'll do whatever it takes to help her to find closure. I did send her a letter years ago, to apologise and let her know I'd won custody of the twins. I guess she never got it. I guess I should have tried harder to make amends. But, whichever way I look at it, the least I can do is go to the wedding. Not because I have any feelings left for her but because I owe her. Question is: will you come with me?'

There was a million-squillion-dollar question if ever there was one. Could she survive three days in the Algarve with

Joe? Forget days—what about the nights? What about the posing-as-loving-girlfriend factor?

Emotions swirled round Imogen's stomach and questions whirled around her brain. Overriding everything was the instinct just to say yes. Because her heart was torn by what Joe had told her and the tragedy he'd gone through. Because her chest warmed with admiration for the way he had fought to look after his sisters, his decision to take on a responsibility far beyond his years. And because she was damn sure Leila wasn't as injured as all that—something was off…she was sure of it.

But somehow she had to retain perspective.

She released his hand and picked up a piece of pizza—more for show than out of hunger. 'I'm not sure lying to Leila is the way forward. You'd be better to talk it all through.'

A barely repressed shudder greeted this suggestion—she'd swear his gills had paled further.

'Wouldn't work. I've tried for the past three weeks to convince her I'm perfectly happy as I am and that she has no need to feel bad. I've got nowhere. Leila needs to see me gallop off into the sunset to my own Happy Ever After.'

Maybe he had a point—talking to Leila did sound pointless. She seemed determined to see things her way. Mind you, so did Joe—he seemed unable to see that his behaviour, whilst not right, had been motivated by grief.

'Fair enough. But why me? There must be women queuing up to go with you—especially to the wedding of the decade. You could take anyone.'

'I don't want to take *anyone*—I want to take you.'

Her heart skipped a beat. 'Why?'

'Because I don't exactly have a list of women I can ask to pose as my girlfriend. And if I hire someone I risk them going to the press—this wedding is big news. I trust you not to do that.'

There was a daft, puppy dog aspect of her that pricked up its ears at any approval. Gave his words a significance they didn't have. The man was her boss and he had the power to make or break Langley. To give him credit, she knew he wouldn't use that to sway her decision—but there was every chance he'd sack her if she ran round betraying him to the press. Hell, she wouldn't blame him.

'Imogen? Yay or nay?'

Think, Imo.

It was a stupid idea for so very many reasons. Such as... 'What about Paris?'

His face shuttered: features immobile, eyes hard. 'What about Paris?'

'Won't it be...awkward?'

'Nope. The past few days have been fine, haven't they?'

Only because they'd become so immersed in work that somehow the awkwardness, the anger and the coldness of the morning after had thawed. Even then 'fine' was probably an exaggeration. Because to her own irritation, her own self-contempt, despite her absorption in work desire had strummed, *flared*, clenched at her tummy muscles with each accidental brush of his hand.

She had managed to keep her cool, not betrayed that desire by so much as a glance, but even so three days and nights in Joe's company would be akin to taking up fire-eating as a new career without any training. It wasn't just stupid—it was crazy.

'Yes. But you're proposing we act as a couple at a wedding. It's a bit different from working together in a boardroom.'

'It won't be a problem.'

As if just because he said so it would be so.

'I've never broken my One Night Only rule and I have no intention of starting now. You were pretty clear that you didn't want a repeat performance either. We agreed one night; we've had one night. I can't see an issue.'

Yet for a fraction of a second his gaze skittered away as he rubbed his neck—and there was the hint of a tic pulsing in his cheek.

Curiosity rippled inside her, along with a thread of sympathy. 'Is your rule because of what happened with Leila?'

Joe snorted. 'Spare me, Imogen. My relationship decisions have nothing to do with Leila or our split. One-night stands suit me because my priority is my sisters. The last thing they need is me introducing anyone into our circle who may not remain in it. But celibacy isn't my chosen option. Equally I have no desire to hurt anyone. One night means there's no time for hopes to be raised or for a relationship to be a possibility.'

'Oh.' That all made perfect sense, and yet… 'How old are your sisters now?'

'Eighteen.'

His face softened and his lips tilted up into a smile of affectionate pride that touched her.

'They are off travelling for a year. Holly has a place lined up at uni and Tammy wants to get straight into the job market. She's already landed a job in television—' He broke off and shook his head. 'Sorry—you don't want to hear about the girls.'

'Actually, I do,' Imogen said. 'It sounds like you've done a marvellous job, and it's wonderful that you've encouraged them to follow their dreams.'

Live the dream.

Moving on fast… 'But now they're eighteen they won't be so affected by you having a relationship longer than a night with someone.'

'I know that. But now it's about what *I* want—and I don't want the hassle or the commitment of a relationship. I love my sisters, and I'll always be there for them, but right now I'm going to kick back and see what it's like to be not just fancy-free but footloose as well.'

That made perfect sense too—he'd had his twenties turned upside down, been emotionally and fiscally responsible for two grieving young girls. Of course he would avoid further commitment like the avian flu. Yet she couldn't help but wonder if he had been more affected than he realised by Leila.

'Anyway… What's your decision? Three days in the Algarve at the wedding of the year? Surrounded by sunshine and the rich and famous? Showing Steve and Simone and the world that Steve is a dim and distant memory?'

When in doubt, eat pizza.

As she chewed Imogen tried to think. Every sensible bone in her body told her to scream *aargghhh* and run the hell away. But she couldn't—she wasn't made that way. Joe might be a ruthless corporate machine, but it turned out he was a human being too. A man who had undergone tragedy and stepped up to the plate to take on a responsibility beyond his years. Her heart ached for him—for the loss of his parents and all the attendant consequences.

Plus, for reasons she couldn't fully fathom, the thought of abandoning him to the wedding—the thought of him being pursued by a line-up of women on the catch for him—had her teeth on edge. There was also the consideration that this wedding would garner publicity, and she'd be less than human if she didn't want to cock a snook at all the people pitying her for Steve's defection.

So what was holding her back, really? Fear that she'd rip all his clothes off? That wouldn't happen. She'd learnt her lesson in Paris—realised that lust truly was dangerous and that all her theories were bang on the nail.

Joe didn't tick any boxes on her tick-list and as such he was off-limits.

'I'll do it,' she said.

His lips curved up into a smile that creased his eyes and flipped her tummy.

'Provided we have separate rooms.' No need to test her resolve too much.

'Separate beds. Apparently I have been allocated a twin room in a villa. Leila and Howard are paying for everything for all their guests. I think separate rooms would defeat the purpose of the whole charade.'

'Fair point.'

Joe reached for his tablet. 'I'll email Leila. Explain that I met you recently and it was love at first sight. We spend three days making sure she believes we've fallen for each other. She swans off into the sunset with full closure achieved.'

It all sounded so simple, and yet a faint flicker of foreboding ignited inside her.

'This calls for a celebration,' Joe stated, and strode across the boardroom to the fridge. 'I bought a few bottles of champagne so the office could celebrate if we won the proposal. I think a toast is in order right now.'

Minutes later he handed her a glass of sparkling amber liquid and clinked his glass against hers. Only then did she realise the sheer error of letting herself get so close.

His sculpted chest was just millimetres from her fingers. His warm scent ignited a deep yearning. Images strobed in her brain. Paris. Champagne. Naked Joe. Naked Imogen.

His eyes darkened, his powerful chest rose and fell, and she wondered if his heart was pounding as hard as hers. Then his jaw clenched as he stepped backwards and raised his glass.

'To the Harvey project,' he said. 'And to the Algarve.'

CHAPTER TEN

IMOGEN STARED OUT of the window of the aeroplane and tried to relax. Before her muscles cramped from the strain of keeping the maximum distance from Joe. Why couldn't she focus on the glorious blue of the sky and the wisps of cotton wool cloud? As opposed to the glory of the toned body scant millimetres from her own and the wisps of ten days' worth of dreams that clouded her brain.

Ten days during which she had managed to avoid him at Langley—relieved that he had held a lot of meetings off site, relieved that he'd spent a lot time closeted with Peter and Harry, walking them through the changes he'd made.

Maybe this hadn't been the world's best idea after all. Mel thought she'd lost the plot *and* her marbles, but Imogen had assured her she was in no danger. The irony wasn't lost on her that she had been sucked into helping another man with his ex-girlfriend issues. But Joe wasn't Steve and the situation was different. Imogen wasn't interested in Joe—he had no long-term relationship potential and she certainly didn't trust this damned attraction that had her practically squirming in her seat.

'So,' he said. 'Peter tells me that the Paris apartment is going well?'

'Yup.' This would be the *other* reason why she'd been avoiding Joe. 'Gosh. Look at that cloud. It looks a bit like a dragon, don't you think?'

'Nope.' He turned his torso so that he faced her and didn't so much as glance out of the window. 'He also said that despite my interim report recommending that you work on the project you've refused.'

'That's right.' Realising she'd folded her arms across her chest, she pushed down the absurd defensiveness and met his gaze full-on. 'There's no need. Peter is so excited by Richard's apartment he's back on form, and he and Belinda are working flat-out. Harry is back part-time and keeping an iron fist on finance, just as your report stated. Plus, there's been an awful lot of admin work to do—especially with all the new procedures you've recommended. So I appreciate your suggestion but I've decided that isn't the way forward for me. From now on I'm a PA and nothing more.'

An ominous frown creased his brow. 'Why?'

'Because…'

Because her time with Joe had terrified her on all sorts of levels and she'd run screaming back into her comfort zone and barricaded all the doors.

'I want to concentrate on streamlining my job properly. Also I need to focus on other aspects of my life. Like finding a place to live, thinking about my future.'

The future she had been in danger of forgetting. The nice, safe, secure one with her tick-list man.

His lips tightened and his eyebrows slashed into the start of a scowl.

'*Anyhoo*,' she said brightly. 'All in all it has been a very busy few days, so I think I'll catch some sleep.'

As if.

But at least closing her eyes put an end to the conversation. It had been tough enough to explain her decision to Peter—almost torturous not to get involved in the project itself. But her resolve had been bolstered when she'd heard Belinda on the phone to her husband, explaining night after night that she had to work late, seen her harassed expression when her child-minder had let her down. All a timely reminder of what could happen if you let a job take over your life. That was not for her.

Forcing herself to breathe evenly and remain still, Imogen kept her eyes firmly closed for the seemingly endless remainder of the journey. Relief arrived when the plane finally began its descent and she could legitimately stretch her cramped muscles.

'Nice rest?' Joe asked, a quirk of his lips expressing scepticism.

'Lovely, thank you.' She could only hope her nose hadn't stretched a centimetre or so. 'I can't believe I'm in the Algarve!'

Still hard to believe even when they descended the steps and a definitely non-British sun kissed her shoulders with glorious warmth as they headed for the airport terminal.

Once they had successfully negotiated passport control, customs, and collected their luggage Imogen looked round. 'What happens now?'

'According to my email from the very efficient wedding planner there will be a car to take us to the villa.' Joe glanced round. 'There we go.'

Following the direction of his finger, Imogen saw a man in a chauffeur's cap and suit holding up a card emblazoned with. 'Leila and Howie's guests'.

As they approached they saw a few others headed the same way. Imogen eyed them, a lump of doubt forming in her tummy. 'They look very glam,' she whispered. 'I'm not sure I'll fit in.'

Joe shrugged. 'And that's a problem because…?'

Before she could answer they had reached the chauffeur, whose name-tag identified him as Len.

'Joe McIntyre and Imogen Lorrimer.'

Len scanned his list and then shook his head. 'You're down for a different car.' He glanced round and pointed. 'Luis will be looking after you.'

'Senhor McIntyre—Senhorita Lorrimer?'

Imogen smiled at the young man who beamed at them as he pushed an overlong lock of dark hair from his forehead.

'I am Luis. I am one of the wedding planners and I will do my best to answer any questions you have about the timetable and I will deal with all your requirements. But first come this way and I will take you to your wonderful accommodation for your stay in the Algarve. All, of course, courtesy of the bride and groom.'

He paused for breath and then smiled again.

'The car is this way. I will take you the motorway route as you will want time to get ready for the ceremony. But there will be lovely scenery towards the end of the trip.'

Imogen glanced at Joe as they climbed into the four-wheel drive car. What was he thinking? It was impossible to tell from his expression but he must be feeling something. The one love of his life, the woman who had driven him to desperation—even if he was over her, even if he hadn't seen her for seven years—was getting married.

None of her business—she was sucked in enough; she couldn't risk getting further involved. That way led madness.

It was best if she concentrated solely on the scenery for the rest of the journey. So as the car glided down the motorway and then wound its way along bendy valley roads she inhaled the sweet breeze and soaked in the greens of the verdure outside until Luis said, 'Nearly there.'

Her vision didn't yield so much as a hut, let alone a villa, and Imogen frowned as Luis turned down a dirt track. 'Wow. So the villa is really secluded, then?'

'Villa?' Luis said. 'No, no—did no one email you?'

'No,' Joe growled. 'Should they have?'

'Yes. You see, all the singletons have been assigned the

villas. You have been given a yurt. You will *love* it. Full
of luxury and romance. It is five-star.'

The scenery became so much irrelevant colour and the
brilliant sunshine faded as Imogen struggled for breath.
'A *yurt*?' she coughed out.

'Do not worry. This is a state-of-the-art yurt. All mod-
cons. Leila and Howard have had them specially put up
for the occasion. You will be able to fall asleep together,
gazing up at the stars.'

Tension ricocheted from Joe's body and no doubt col-
lided with hers; in fact their mingled tension could probably power a rocket. All the way to the ruddy stars.

'Here we are,' Luis said cheerfully, apparently oblivi-
ous to the atmosphere as he parked the car and turned to
look at them. 'Howard was very particular about your accommodation, so I hope I can report back to him that you
are happy. Yes?'

Oh, hell and damnation. They were supposed to be a
loved-up couple and Imogen had no doubt that Howard
Kreel would much rather that was *exactly* what they were.
It couldn't be much fun for the groom, having his bride's
ex-boyfriend there for 'closure'.

This was clearly her cue to be adoring, when in actual
fact the desire to strangle Joe with her bare hands was
making her palms itch. 'Of course we're happy,' she said.
'How would it be possible *not* to be happy? Don't you
agree, sweetheart?'

'Absolutely,' Joe said, with a credible attempt at enthusiasm and an overdose of heartiness. As if Joe had ever
been *hearty* in his life. 'Imogen and I are sure to appreciate every second of our stay.'

'Excellent.' Luis sprang out of the car and opened Imogen's door. 'Then I'll take you on a guided tour of the site
and leave you to it.'

Imogen tried to appreciate the fairytale beauty of the

site—she really did. It was a good few steps up even from a *glamp*site. Lord knew how much it must have cost to convert the area so spectacularly. Tipis and luxury tents dotted the area—all individually decorated and all, Luis assured them again, equipped with a variety of mod-cons. Two large wooden huts had also been constructed.

'There is the bar and the dining area. Meals and refreshments will be available all day.'

In addition to what money could buy was the wealth of nature's offerings—the colourful flowers, the vibrant vegetation, the lap of water from a small brook that wound its way down a rocky precipice and then meandered through the lush lime-green meadow.

And there in a secluded corner...

'Here we are,' Luis announced, gesturing at a pink canvas palace. 'You have guaranteed privacy. All the details about the wedding and the reception and the available activities are in a folder inside. The coach will arrive at four to take you to the beach ceremony.'

'Fabulous. Thank you *so* much, Luis,' Imogen trilled, forcing her lips upward, keeping the smile...aka rictus... in place as she watched his departing back.

Two more strides and Luis had climbed into the four-seater.

'Not! This is *not* fabulous, Joe. Look at it. It's got *turrets*! It's the yurt of love. What happened to the twin beds in a villa?'

'Yes, well, I obviously got upgraded from singleton to one of the loved-up people.' He thrust a hand through his hair. 'Let's not panic until we've actually looked inside.'

'Fine.' Imogen tugged the canvas door open. 'Um...'

Pink canvas walls were draped with beaded curtains and gauzy material. There were tasselled cushions, luxury pile rugs, an overstuffed sofa, a dressing table...and an enormous sleigh bed.

Below a porthole.

With a view of the stars.

For a fleeting second she wished that there could be a rerun of Paris—another rash decision to break the rules. But she knew that wasn't possible. Once was fine—could be chalked up to a magical experience. Twice… That was way too dangerous and she wouldn't go there. Couldn't go there for the sake of her own sanity.

She was *not* going to end up bedazzled, befuddled and controlled by lust.

Turning to Joe, she swept her hand towards the bed. '*Now* can I panic?'

Joe exhaled heavily and forced his features to neutral. What had he ever done to deserve this? A twin room in a populated villa would have been tough, but manageable. Worst-case scenario: he'd have stayed up in the lounge playing video games. All night.

There was nowhere to go in a yurt.

Chill. He needed to chill. He was a ruthless corporate businessman, for goodness' sake—not an adolescent.

Plus he had no one to blame but himself; this whole jaunt had been *his* damn fool idea. Now he would just have to suck it up.

'No need…' He stopped and cleared his throat, forced more words past the knot of panic in his throat. 'No need to freak out. I'll sleep on the sofa; you can have the bed.'

Rocking back on his heels, he swept a final glance around the tent and rubbed the back of his neck.

'I guess you need to change, so I'll leave you to it.'

Fresh air—that was what he needed. Fresh air and exercise. Perhaps if he walked a very, very long way he'd walk off the desire that urged him to turn round, rip open the door of the yurt and throw Imogen down onto the bed. Walk off the desire.

Master plan, McIntyre. But it was the only one he had…
It didn't work worth a damn.

An hour later, as he approached the yurt, anticipation unfurled in his chest. And when he stepped into the pink canvas bubble he stopped in his tracks. Because Imogen looked so beautiful she robbed his lungs of air. Her dark hair rode her shoulders in sleek glossy waves; a floaty floral dress gave her beauty an ethereal edge.

She rose from the dressing table and faced him, her lips tilted in an almost shy smile as she spread out her arms and gave a twirl, the orange and red flowers of the dress vibrant as they swirled around her.

'Do you think this is all right?' she asked. 'I chose it myself—no help from Mel, no ulterior motive. Just because I like it. But now I'm worried that it's not glam enough.'

'I don't think that's a problem,' he managed. Though his blood pressure might be approaching the turreted roof.

'You sure?'

'One hundred per cent. You look beautiful. I promise.'

Silence enveloped them; awareness hummed in the air. Time to distract himself.

Keeping his movements casual, he headed for the sofa and picked up a leatherbound folder.

'That must be the itinerary Luis mentioned,' Imogen said, her voice slightly high as she sat down.

'Yup.' He stared down at the words and forced his brain to make sense of them. 'So, as we know, after the ceremony there's a Bond-themed party on a yacht. We'll need to take a change of clothes with us. Then tomorrow there are various activities we can do. Leila and Howard will have left for their honeymoon, but they want all their guests to stay and have fun.'

'Activities?' Imogen looked up and there was genuine enthusiasm on her face as she no doubt worked out a way to avoid his company for the day. 'That sounds like a great idea. What sort of activities?'

Joe scanned the list. 'Sightseeing, beach yoga, surfing and…'

'And what?'

'There's an art class run by Michael Mallory, who is a lecturer at one of London's top art colleges. You should do that.'

Imogen narrowed her eyes. 'You don't give up, do you?'

'No. I've seen how talented you are—seems a shame for it to go to waste.'

'That is not your decision to make.'

'Agreed… But I just don't get why you are being so damn stubborn about this.'

For a second unease pricked his conscience. Why did it matter so much to him? Hell, it was way better to have this conversation right now than dwell on all the other things they could do in the Yurt of Love.

'Now is as good a time as any for you to tell me. No excuses—no need to nap.'

'I *did* need a nap.'

'Rubbish! No one sleeps with their body completely still and radiating tension. You were ducking out of a proper explanation of why you refused to go along with my report and help out on Richard's apartment. And please spare me the *I can't do any art because I need to move* crap.'

'It's the truth.' One defiant swivel and she presented her back to him, leaning forward to pick up a lipstick and peer into the heart-shaped gilded mirror. 'So I'll give the lesson a miss.'

'Shame.' Joe leant against the cushioned back rest and picked up the folder again. '"Michael Mallory: esteemed lecturer and mentor to Justin Kinley, Myra Olsten and Becca Farringham, all of whom exploded on to the art scene after graduation. Michael has planned an intense day in which you will learn how to express your artistic instincts and find your own definite artistic voice. This kind of near one-on-one tuition is an incredible chance to learn from a master and—"'

'Stop!' Imogen spun on the chair to face him, her chest rising and falling as she jabbed a mascara wand in the air. 'Just stop—OK?'

'Why? I'm just telling you what you're missing.'

'I get it. OK? I get what I'm missing and I'm good with it.'

Only she wasn't. Not by a long shot. He could see the sparkle of tears in her eyes even as she blinked fiercely. Sense her anger and frustration as she clenched her hands round the edge of her seat and inhaled deeply.

'Imo, sweetheart. You're *not* good with it.'

He stood, strode over the canvas floor and dropped to his haunches in front of her, covering her hands with his.

'Tell me. C'mon. I'm sorry I went on at you but I've seen your talent. That proposal—you made the sketches come alive. I could see the glitter of the mirror, feel the softness of the sheets, smell the freshly baked baguettes.'

'They were just a few pencil and charcoal sketches.'

'They were a lot more than that.' He shook his head. 'I don't get it, Imogen. Why don't you take the project further? I've seen how absorbed you've been, how much it matters to you.'

He had seen her frustration if it hadn't been perfect— the way she'd thrown crumpled bits of paper at the bin— seen the ink streaks on her forehead, the forgotten cups of tea and coffee, the food he'd forced her to eat.

'And that's exactly the problem!' she said.

'Meaning?'

For a moment she hesitated, and then a small reluctant smile tugged at her lips. 'I'm guessing you won't let up until I explain?'

'Nope.'

She leant back against the dresser and inhaled an audible breath. 'I told you my parents' marriage is less than stellar?'

Joe nodded.

'I didn't explain why. The main reason is my dad. He's an artist, and he's dedicated his life to his art even though he's barely sold anything. It's an obsession with him—more important than my mum, more important than me. Mum did *everything*. Worked at any job she could get to pay the bills and put food on the table. She wanted to study, to go to uni, but somehow it never happened. It couldn't because Dad wouldn't go and get a job, it was always, "When I get recognised, then it will all change."'

Her shoulders hitched in a shrug.

'Mum couldn't even leave me with him when she was at work, because he got so absorbed in his work he forgot me. It consumed him. I don't want that in my life.'

His throat tightened as he saw the pain in her eyes. So much made sense now: her desire for a job that didn't challenge her, her need for a partner who pulled his weight.

'Just because your father lost perspective it doesn't mean you would.'

'Not a risk I'm willing to take. And even if I were I couldn't do that to Mum. She had such high hopes for me. She wanted me to be a lawyer or an accountant. Make something of my life...do all the stuff she missed out on. When it turned out I couldn't achieve that she was devastated... I can't disappoint her even more.'

'But surely what your mum wants most for you is for you to be happy? You should talk to her about this. You can't live your life for your parents.'

Imogen shook her head. 'I'm not. Sure, Mum steered me away from art at every turn—but I don't blame her for that. I don't want to be bitten by the bug. Mum *does* want me to be happy and so do I. I know what I want from my life—I want to be secure, settled and comfortable. I want a nice husband and two point four kids. Maybe a Labrador and a white picket fence. The happy bonus is that I won't make my mother miserable, watching her daughter follow the same road as her husband.'

'The less than happy price is that you miss out on something you love.'

'Then it's a price I'm willing to pay.'

'Even to the point of not taking up art as a *hobby*?'

'I can't.' A small shake of her head as she looked at him almost beseechingly. 'I've realised that these past weeks. I did love doing Richard's proposal, I did enjoy working on projects for Peter, but you saw what happened. I became obsessed.'

'That was one proposal—with a deadline. And you don't have a family yet.'

'Doesn't matter. I have to draw a line under it now.' As if suddenly realising his hands still covered hers, she pulled them away. 'Do you understand?'

'Yes, I understand.'

Her words pulled a nerve taut. Years ago, after his parents' death, that had been his exact decision. With two grief-stricken sisters to look after and a company to try and sort out—responsibilities that had surpassed his own dreams—he'd drawn a line under his surfing career. He'd taken his board out one last time—and the memory of the cool breeze, the tang of salt, the roll of the waves was etched on his soul in its significance.

'But I don't agree.'

He rose to his feet and looked down at her. Lord knew he did know how she felt—maybe that was why he was reacting so strongly to Imogen's decision. But he'd had no choice. His sisters were his priority—that was an absolute, and he had no regrets as to his decision. But this...

this was different, and he wished—*so* wished—there was some way to show Imogen that.

'Your talent—your art—is a fundamental part of you that you're shutting down.'

'Maybe. But by shutting it down I get to be the person I want to be.' Her lips curved into a small smile. 'It's truly lovely of you to care, and I appreciate it, Joe, but I made this decision long ago—it's the sensible option. And I'm all about the sensible.'

Turning, she picked up the abandoned mascara wand and leant forward to peer at her reflection.

Only she *wasn't* 'all about the sensible'. He'd seen Imogen Lorrimer at her least sensible and she'd been vibrant and alive and happy.

It's truly lovely of you to care.

Her words echoed round his brain and set off alarm bells. Caring was not on his agenda. Time to back off— Imogen's life was hers. He'd had his say and now it was time to join the Sensible Club.

'Have it your way,' he said.

CHAPTER ELEVEN

IMOGEN SWALLOWED PAST the gnarl of emotion in her throat; she didn't even *know* Leila or Howard, and yet the sight of them repeating their vows had tears prickling the backs of her eyelids.

In a gown that clung to her in diaphanous folds of ivory and lace Leila radiated bridal joy—her smile could probably illuminate the whole of the Algarve. But it wasn't that which touched Imogen most—it was the way Howard looked at his bride. Such love, such adoration, such pride that it was little wonder Imogen's chest ached.

Hollywood, eat your heart out. Imogen, get a grip.

Maybe she was overreacting like this because the setting was so damn movie-like: the golden sand, the lap of waves and the glow of the setting sun that streaked flames of orange across the dusky sky.

What she needed to remember was that this was a moment of time—not a happy-ever-after. Look at her parents: she had pored over their wedding photos as a child, in an attempt to work out how such rosy happiness could have evaporated into screaming and bitterness.

Her parents' dreams had crumbled to dust, their radiance no more than sex and foolish hope. Proof-positive that a marriage based on lust did not work—a marriage between two incompatible people did not work. But a marriage based on a tick-list would. Imogen was sure of it.

There was a collective gasp as Howard lifted his wife's veil and kissed her. As Leila slid one slender arm around his neck Imogen cast a surreptitious look at Joe. Did he mind? Was he revisiting the past, wondering what would have happened if Leila had agreed to marry him all those years ago?

Surely not. He didn't look like a man harbouring thoughts of the past—if anything he looked faintly bored. Unless, of course, it was all a façade—Joe was hardly a man to wear his heart on the sleeve of his grey suit, and that was even assuming he *had* one.

'You OK?' she asked under cover of the applause that had broken out as Howard and Leila continued their lip-lock.

'Why wouldn't I be?'

'You loved her once—whatever your reasons, you wanted to commit a lifetime to her.'

Broad shoulders hitched. 'I'm happy for her—happy that she is happy. That the damage I did has been mitigated. No more than that.' He glanced around. 'Come on. It's the receiving line. So don't forget to turn on the adoring look.'

'I think you've forgotten something.'

'What?'

'It's a two-way street. You have to look adoringly at me too.'

And she had to remember that this was fake. Needed to dismiss the wistfulness that wisped through her brain at the thought that Leila and Simone got the real McCoy version of the adoring look and she was stuck with the false one.

Joe raised his eyebrows, a small smile playing on his lips, and all thoughts of wistfulness blew away, to be replaced by far more dangerous memories of the havoc those lips could cause.

'You think I can't do adoring?' he asked.

'I'm finding it hard to imagine.'

'Watch and learn, Imogen. Watch and learn.'

His cool broad fingers grasped hers and Imogen bit her lip to hold in her gasp. It was their first contact in days and her skin reacted like a parched plant in the depths of the Sahara to rain.

A little flicker of envy ignited in her as they approached Leila—even the stunning photos that graced the celebrity mags hadn't done her justice. Long blonde hair shimmered under her veil, exotic green eyes lit up as they rested on Joe, and her smile demonstrated the slant of perfect cheekbones and the curve of glossy provocative lips.

'J!' she exclaimed in a melodious yet husky voice that fitted the setting perfectly.

Any second now birds would swoop from the sky and land on her and everyone would break into song.

Not that Imogen cared. Much. So who knew why a mixture of jealousy and mortification seared her insides as Leila threw her arms around Joe before stepping back and raising a hand to cup his jaw?

'It's so very good to see you, J. I do appreciate you coming.'

Imogen tried not to clench her nails into Joe's palm and made an attempt to access the voice of reason. Leila was the bride—no way was she hitting on Joe. Or should she say *J*? *All* ex-girlfriends didn't have an agenda to win back their boyfriends. This was closure. Yet…damn it… she wasn't imagining that proprietorial look on Leila's face.

Joe stepped back and put an arm around Imogen's waist, squeezed her against him. 'Good to see you too, Leila— and congratulations. This is Imogen.'

Imogen blinked—was that *Joe's* voice? Low and tender and…well…*adoring*? As if he were introducing someone special and precious?

The bride's perfect smile froze a touch—she was sure of it.

'Imogen. I am so happy to meet you. You and I must have a proper girl-to-girl chat at the reception.'

Well, wouldn't *that* be fun? 'Super,' Imogen said, managing a smile as they moved along to stand in front of Howard.

'Joe. My man.' The groom slapped Joe on the back with what looked like excessive force. 'Thanks for coming along, dude,' he said. 'It means a lot to Leila—which is why I told her of *course* I didn't mind. Oh, and from one surfing dude to another—make sure you take your board out while you're here.'

Joe's lean body tensed next to hers and Imogen glanced up at him. Surfing dude? Joe was a *surfing dude*? Could Howard be mixing him up with someone else? There was nothing in Joe's face to indicate his thoughts; his features could have been carved from granite.

'Imogen.' Howard grasped her hands. 'It is so very nice to meet you and to know that Joe is in good hands. Hope you like the yurt?'

'It's—' Before Imogen could reply she saw Leila's head turn.

'But I put Joe and Imogen in the villa, sweetie.'

'I changed the plan, sugar puff. Paid a bundle for that yurt—shame for it to go to waste.'

A small frown creased Leila's brow before she smiled her radiant smile. 'Wonderful idea.'

'It's incredible,' Imogen chipped in, before they moved along to where the bride's and groom's parents awaited.

'Phew…' She whistled as they walked away from the line. 'I don't think you're exactly Mr Popular—with Howard's family or Leila's.'

'No big surprise, given the way I treated Leila.'

Imogen frowned. 'I'm not sure that's the problem.'

'What do you mean?'

'I get the idea they're worried that Leila still has feel-

ings for you. To be honest, if I was your real girlfriend so
would I be.'

Come to that, even as his fake girlfriend she wasn't
happy about the idea.

Joe shook his head. 'That doesn't make sense. This is
Leila's wedding day—she hasn't seen me in seven years.
And, believe me, she can't possibly have any good memo-
ries of how we parted.'

'I suppose.'

Joe had a point—maybe her imagination had gone into
overdrive. So affected by Steve's defection to Simone that
she found bugbears where there weren't any. But...

She shrugged. 'Well, bear it in mind as a possibility.'

Before Joe could answer Luis waved at them and headed
over. 'It was a beautiful ceremony, yes?'

'Absolutely.'

'And now your change of clothes is in the beach huts.
If you come this way, and once you have changed please
head for the yacht. Women this way—men that way.'

Joe stepped onto the garlanded deck of the yacht and
blinked at the dazzling array of glittering disco balls and
spinning lights that strobed the deck with multicoloured
lights. Men in tuxedos and women in various Bond girl
costumes chattered, their voices mingling with the Bond-
themed music. As he scanned the crowd for Imogen he realised that he had no idea what she would be wearing. Not
that it mattered—he would know her by her stance, her
glorious shape, the sweep of her dark hair.

'You must be Joe,' a breathy voice proclaimed.

Before he could sidestep her a curvy petite woman had
launched herself at him on a wave of overpowering perfume.

'Oh, my! You're every bit as gorgeous as Leila said. I'm
Katrina. Part of your line-up. I know you've come with

some other woman, but I wanted you to see what you're missing, sugar.'

Was she for real? 'No need, thanks. I'm—'

'Oh, come on, darlin'…no man can resist me. Just one little kiss.'

As Katrina pressed her over-glossed lips to his Joe looked over the top of the petite blonde's head to see Imogen walking straight towards them, her gown a swirl of Bohemian tangerine-orange. Her smile dropped from her lips and she faltered for a heartbeat as she took in the scene. Then her lips tightened, and if she could have lasered him with her glare he'd be dead by now.

Taking Katrina firmly by the arms, he hoisted her away from him.

'I'm taken,' he finished.

Katrina turned on one stiletto heel and gave a little giggle. 'Dear me. Caught red-handed. Catch you later, Joe honey.'

'Why don't you chase after her, *Joe honey*?' Imogen asked.

The cool sarcasm caught him on the raw. Surely she didn't believe he'd instigated that interlude?

'Don't mind me.'

'I don't want to chase after her. That was Katrina. One of the line-up you're here to protect me from.'

'Didn't look to me as though you needed protection at all.' Imogen emitted a mirthless laugh as she gestured to his pants pocket. 'Apart from the type that comes in foil packets. And no doubt you've got plenty of those handy in your wallet.'

A flash of anger stabbed him as he leant back against the railings. Did she really think so little of him?

'You don't think you're overreacting a touch?'

'I'm the one who found you with a woman draped all

over you, her tongue practically stuck down your throat. And you think I'm overreacting?'

'Yes, I do. Nice imagery. Even better point: Katrina *was* draped over me—believe me, short of dodging her and letting her fall flat on her face there wasn't much I could do.'

'Oh, please. That is ridiculous—a big, strong man like you couldn't defend himself? I'm sure you have plenty of moves to avoid women of all shapes and sizes, and Katrina is hardly wrestler material. From where I was standing you looked pretty happy.'

Shaking her head so that the orange flowers woven into her hair vibrated, she hoisted her palms in a get-away-from-me gesture.

'I cannot *believe* I could have been so stupid as to come to this wedding with you. I actually bought that whole spiel you gave me.'

What the hell…?

'Spiel? It wasn't a spiel. I told you the truth.' Which hadn't exactly been a picnic for him.

'*Hah!* I just had the dubious pleasure of witnessing "the truth".'

Frustration mixed with bewilderment and he expelled a sigh. 'Imogen. If I wanted to get involved with Katrina why would I have brought you to the wedding at all?'

'Maybe you hadn't realised how attractive Katrina would be. Maybe you're regretting bringing me.' Imogen's blue-grey eyes narrowed and she clicked her fingers. 'Or maybe this is all a ploy to make Leila jealous. What are you hoping for, Joe? That she'll realise that she still loves you?'

For a second sheer disbelief froze him to the spot. Then… 'Enough!'

Propelled by sheer anger, Joe stepped forward and pulled her into his arms.

'Stop it!' Slamming her palms on his chest, she leant

back against his hold. 'No need to kiss *me*. Leila already believes we are an item.'

'Never mind that,' he growled. 'I'm going to show you what a real kiss is—and then you can understand that I was *not* kissing Katrina.'

The idea that she really believed he was such a bastard made his blood simmer in his veins and he sealed her mouth in one harsh swoop. He revelled in the lushness of her lips, the taste of mint and strawberry. Her body stilled and then she tangled her fingers in his hair. The angry stroke of her tongue against his sent a shudder through him and he pulled her tight against him, so she could feel his body's instant savage reaction.

OK. Stop now, Joe. Whilst you can. Point made.

Breaking the kiss, he stared down at her as their ragged breaths mingled in the evening breeze. *'That's* a real kiss,' he rasped. 'Do you really believe I'd bring you here as my guest and then go off with someone else? *Really?'*

Her slim shoulders lifted in a shrug. 'Why wouldn't you? If it was a tactic in your strategy to win Leila back, I'm sure you are more than ruthless enough to do just that.'

'What strategy? I do not want to win Leila back. Even if I did I'm not a complete bastard. I have too much respect for you to treat you as a pawn. I am at this wedding for all the reasons I told you. I have no interest in Katrina. I am *not* Steve. You are not second-best. It's your call whether you believe me or not.'

Before she could answer he saw Luis, wending his way through the tables towards them. 'Ah, here you are,' he said with a smile. 'Leila sent me to find you. She'd like a chat with Imogen.'

Joe bit back the urge to tell Luis to tell Leila to take a hike; he and Imogen were in the midst of an important conversation. It mattered to him that Imogen believed him.

Imogen, on the other hand, practically leapt towards

Luis, clearly relieved to be let off the conversational hook. 'Of course. I'll come straight away.' As Luis started to thread his way through the crowds she turned and murmured, 'Don't worry, Joe. I'll stick to my part of the bargain. *Whatever* your motivations for wanting me to.'

CHAPTER TWELVE

'ALONG HERE,' LUIS said, and led Imogen away from the thronged deck, where people shimmied and twisted to the beat of the music. Imogen followed on automatic, still processing what had just happened with Joe; trying to work out what to believe.

Instinct bade her to accept Joe's version of events, but her instincts were hardly the most reliable—she'd trusted Steve implicitly and that hadn't exactly ended well. Worse, it could be that her instincts had been skewed by that kiss, her brain deceived by a heady cloud of lust. Her lips—hell, her whole body—still buzzed from the aftershock.

The noise from the deck faded as she followed Luis down some stairs and into a private corridor. *Come on, Imogen—get prepared.* She'd told Joe she'd still play her allocated role—convince Leila that she was Joe's much-loved girlfriend.

Her brain whirled. Did Joe have a point? Why would he have kissed Katrina if he wanted this charade to play out? Because he wanted Leila to realise that he wasn't really in love with Imogen and that he was available? Her temples ached as she tried to work it out.

Luis pushed a door open. 'In here.'

For a mad moment Imogen expected him to announce her, but instead he simply flashed a smile and withdrew. Still, the feeling of being a subject granted an audience, or in this case summoned, persisted.

The spacious conference room was dominated by a

sleek oval cherrywood table, with Leila enthroned at one
end on an ornate chair. She'd removed her veil, and also
the train of her dress, so that now she was encased in a
lace concoction that hit mid-thigh and moulded her model
figure to perfection.

Suddenly the tangerine Bohemian look seemed a fashion disaster—maybe the black diamanté evening dress
would have been better. She shook her head—why was she
even thinking about this now? Maybe it was the slightly
patronising I-am-more-beautiful-than-you-can-ever-be-
and-we-both-know-it look in Leila's green eyes. Shades
of Simone's cornflower-blue orbs, with their I-am-more-
exciting-alluring-and-interesting-than-you-and-Steve-has-
always-loved-me expression.

'Imogen. Thank you for seeing me in private.'

'No problem.' Choking back a sudden surge of hollow
laughter, she tried to smile as she sat down.

'Howard and I are leaving tonight, and before I go I
need to make sure Joe is in good hands.'

'Right. I see.' Or rather… 'Well, actually—no, I don't.
Joe's happiness is not your responsibility.' Unless, of
course, Joe's strategy was working and Leila was having
second thoughts.

The blonde woman settled back on the chair and shook
her head. 'You see, that's where you're wrong. I dashed
Joe's hopes to the ground years ago—spurned his love—
so I do feel that his happiness is very much my responsibility. He *loved* me so much. I was his world and then I
rejected him.'

Hurt touched Imogen and she gritted her teeth, unable
to help wondering what it must feel like to have Joe—cor-
rection, to have *any* man—think she was his world.

'I feel so awful that I broke his heart like that… And
when he looked at me today I saw all that love as though
it had never gone away…could be rekindled in a trice…'

The leaden realisation that she had been right plummeted in Imogen's tummy. Joe *did* still love Leila—she had been right on the money.

Wait. The word lit up her brain in neon and her gut screamed at her to listen to it as her brain replayed his words. *'I have too much respect for you to treat you as a pawn. I am at this wedding for all the reasons I told you.'*

She replayed their conversation over pizza in the Langley boardroom. His voice as he told her the truth about his past: the tragedy and its outcome. The guilt over Leila; his need to make amends.

Finding her voice, she met Leila's emerald-green eyes, tried to read her expression. 'Do you *want* to rekindle Joe's love? Do you still love him?'

'No. Not at all. Howie is the man for me. But now I know for sure Joe still has feelings for me I wanted to talk to you, so we can come up with a strategy to help him get over me.'

The hell with this. There was every possibility that she'd regret this, but somehow it wasn't possible for Imogen to believe that Joe had lied to her. Ruthlessness was one thing; dishonesty was another. Steve had lied to her. Joe hadn't. Not once.

'I think he *has* got over you.'

The words were liberating and oh, so right.

Green eyes blinked at her in sheer incomprehension. 'Darling, I know you want to believe that, but it's simply not true. I saw the look in his eyes when he saw me. I—'

'So did I. Joe told me he's over you and I believe him.'

'Then why hasn't he had a relationship since me?'

'Because he's spent the last seven years bringing up his sisters. You know that.'

'Don't I just? Those twins are devil children. I never understood how he could pick them over me. Without the twins maybe I could have stuck it out. Though I don't know… I remember the first time he dressed up in a suit to go and sort out his dad's company. He didn't look like my Joe any more. He'd changed so much. No more surfing—just dull, dull, dull business stuff. No more photo shoots, no more magazine articles, no more parties and travel… Joe could have been a surfing champion—famous, rich, having a life of freedom and fun. With me. He *knew* that was what I wanted, but he couldn't see sense.'

Surfing again. So it was true. Only Joe had been more than a 'surfing dude'—he'd been a champion, with a glittering career ahead of him. Her heart rended at the image of corporate, suited and booted Joe riding the waves, free and laid-back and happy, before tragedy struck.

'He chose the twins over me. And when I told him I couldn't marry him he heaped abuse on my head. I know it was because he was driven to distraction by my refusal and his love for me, but it *hurt*, Imogen. So much.'

For a few seconds Imogen could only open and close her mouth as sheer disbelief silenced her vocal cords. Joe had given up so much and then achieved so much, without complaint, regret or martyrdom. And this idiot couldn't see *any* of that. Could only see how the world revolved around *her*.

Drawing breath, Imogen tried to do as Joe had asked. 'Joe does feel terrible about how he treated you. He did actually write you a letter, apologising and…'

'*Hah!* I got that letter…'

Imogen stilled, a layer of anger laving the inside of her tummy. 'You *got* that letter? Why didn't you contact Joe?'

'What was the point?' Leila shook her head. 'His letter was full of the twins and how he'd won custody. It was too late for him to change his mind. Otherwise I'd have given him a second chance. If he'd seen reason it may not have been too late for us to recapture our love and—'

'Rubbish. You didn't love Joe. You wanted to hang onto

his board shorts and be carried to fame and fortune. And you didn't care what happened to the twins as long as you got what you wanted.'

'That's not true. If he'd loved me he would have put me first. That's what love is. I was trying to show him how to be happy.'

'Joe asked you to marry him. Spend your life with him. If you loved him wouldn't you have at least thought about it? Even if it was just to help him with the twins?'

Leila threw up her arms. 'Those damned twins.'

'They were people, Leila. Children—*grieving* children. How could Joe have lived with himself if he'd abandoned them?'

'Hooey.'

'Hooey?'

'Yes. Hooey.' Leila nodded in emphasis. 'Joe and I could have had a wonderful future together. He would have made a fortune—not just from surfing but from advertising and endorsements. We would have been as big as any of these football celebrity couples. We could have had it all—hell, by now we could have been on reality TV, with millions in the bank.'

'Is that what Joe wanted?'

'Of course. He loved surfing—and I'd have handled all the other stuff. But then he went and blew it.'

Anger was on a slow burn now, along with a feeling of wonder as to why Joe thought he owed Leila *anything*. 'It wasn't his fault his parents died.'

'No, but he didn't have to let it change everything.'

'But it *did* change everything!'

OK, so she'd yelled, but it had been either that or give in and shake some sense into Leila.

'Leila, you need to wake up and smell the coffee—or iced tea, or whatever. Just for a minute can you *please* try and look at this from a different perspective?'

For a second guilt prodded Imogen. Less than an hour ago she'd been just as bad as Leila, willing to condemn Joe because of her own fears and inadequacies. She had judged him unfairly. Now she could make amends. By standing up for him. And maybe she could achieve something more. Because whether he liked it or not Joe had been affected by his relationship with Leila. Maybe this was Imogen's chance to achieve closure for him. And if that meant bursting Leila's bubble then she'd enjoy every second.

'If Joe had done what you wanted and surfed off into the sunset with you what would have happened to his sisters?'

'Well…they…they would have been fine. He could have visited them, kept in touch. They could have come to stay with us every so often.'

'Visited them where, Leila?'

Red stained the blonde's cheeks. 'There must have been other relatives.'

'Nope.'

'The care system. Or…' Discomfort creased Leila's face.

'You didn't think, did you?' Imogen leant forward and slammed a palm down on the table, hearing the frustration sharpen her voice. 'Or rather you just thought about yourself. If it had been me all those years ago I'd have married him to help him through. I'd have stood by him. He's a good man. Who feels terrible about the way he behaved to you all those years ago. He believes he blighted your life. *Did* he?'

The green eyes skittered away. 'I would dream about his anguished face…his words of anger would echo in my eardrums.'

'Leila. This is real life. *Please*. There is a good man up there, beating himself up because he thinks he did you damage. A man who gave up his dream to look after his sisters. A man who built a new life for them and him.'

A man she had accused unfairly and owed an apology to herself. But that could come later—now her chest ached as she held her breath and hoped that her words had had some effect.

There was a long silence as Leila's glossy painted mouth opened and closed, and to Imogen's surprise she saw the green eyes swim with tears.

'Oh, hell,' Leila said. 'Double hell. Now my mascara is running.' A small sniff and suddenly she looked a whole lot more accessible. 'You're right.' She gusted out a sigh. 'I'm behaving appallingly. I've always felt terrible about the way I left Joe. I was young and shallow and, truth be told, I don't believe Joe and I really loved each other. I loved being a surfer chick and he loved having a hot blonde girlfriend.'

'That's OK.' Surprise and a sudden leap of elation at the knowledge that her instincts had been right after all fizzed in Imogen's tummy.

'But that doesn't mean I should have deserted him. And now—because I don't want to face what an outright bitch I was, and I certainly don't want Howard to know—I've rewritten history to suit myself. Without giving Joe a thought. I'm sorry.'

Imogen shook her head. 'It's not me you owe the apology to.'

'You think I should talk to Joe?'

'Yes, I do.' Imogen smiled—whatever her faults, it had taken guts for Leila to acknowledge the truth and want to make amends. 'That way you can both have closure.'

'And I can get on with doing what I'm best at. Being adored and fêted and looked after.'

'I think that's the bride's prerogative. Truly, Leila, I wish you and Howard very happy.'

'We will be, darling. And, Imogen?'

'Yes?'

'I'm sorry I tried to put you in the villa and gave you all those evil vibes. I know what it looks like, but I'm really not interested in Joe. I love my husband. It's just…'

'Just what?'

Leila sighed. 'I suppose I was so caught up in this story I'd concocted, about being the woman Joe would never be able to get over, that it was a bit of a shock to hear about you and then see that he is genuinely happy. But I'm glad he's found real love—truly.'

'Leila, I—'

'No, really. I know he doesn't love easily, but I can see how much he adores you. I'm glad he's found the happiness that I have. I *do* love Howie, so very much. And that's why I'll tell him the unvarnished truth. *After* the honeymoon!'

Leila winked and rose to her feet, and Imogen couldn't help but smile as she followed her out of the room.

Once back on deck, Imogen found a secluded spot and leant against the railings as Leila approached Howard, had a quiet word with him, and then kissed him with a long, lingering embrace before she headed over to Joe. Minutes later the two of them headed off the deck.

Imogen turned and faced out to sea, hoping that the long overdue conversation would help Joe to cut himself a little slack. The sound of the waves lapping against the yacht made her heart suddenly ache. Giving up surfing must have been tough for Joe, and it made his insistence that she try out that art lesson make way more sense.

For a while she lost herself in a daydream, trying to imagine a younger, more carefree Joe, master of the waves, travelling to different competitions, sponsored, fêted, and doing something he loved.

But he'd given that dream up—and done so without martyring himself or making his sisters feel bad. He'd done what Eva Lorrimer had been unable to do—how could she not admire him for that?

The hairs on the nape of her neck rose to attention: a sure sign that Joe was in the vicinity.

'Hey.'

The warmth of his body was right next to her as he leant back against the rails so he was looking directly at her.

'Hey.' She smiled at him tentatively 'How did it go?'

Joe opened his mouth and closed it again, poleaxed by the sheer beauty of her smile. The reddish-orange of her kaftan dress was vivid in the dusk, her eyes bright with a warm, questioning look.

'It was...great.' He felt as though he'd shed a weight he'd barely even known he carried. 'Thank you. Leila told me what you said in there. If you hadn't championed me we'd both have gone on looking back from a skewed angle. Now we've sorted out the good memories and got the bad ones into perspective—and that feels good. So I'll say it again. Thank you.' He paused. 'I take it I'm off the Katrina hook as well?'

'Yes.' She blew out air and brushed her fringe from her forehead. 'I'm sorry. It's just that's exactly what Simone did to get Steve back. Turned up at some party with another man on her arm. He made a beeline for her. Worst thing is, I trusted him—thought he was aiming for closure. Turned out the only place he was aiming for was the bedroom, and I didn't realise. He two-timed me for months and I didn't have a clue. When Steve finally told me the truth he told me I was monochrome, grey, whilst Simone lit up his world.' Slim shoulders hitched. 'But it doesn't mean I should have painted you the same colour!'

'Then he must have been blind. You aren't grey and you aren't monochrome. You're Imogen Lorrimer, smart and beautiful—hell, you practically light up the yacht. I promise.'

For a long moment she stared at him, and his heart

twisted as he saw doubt wrestle with her desire to believe him. His feet itched with the urge to get hold of Steve and kick him round the town for what he'd done to Imogen, undermining whatever self-belief her mother had left her with.

'Thank you.'

'You're very welcome.'

Awareness flickered into being. The strains of music and the raised voices faded and all there seemed to be in the world was Imogen—so beautiful, so damned kissable. *Snap out of it, Joe.*

He forced a smile to his lips. 'Hey, we could start a mutual admiration society.'

Imogen blinked as if to break the spell. 'I'll drink to that.'

'I can take a hint. Hold that thought.'

Joe glanced around and waved at a passing waiter, who came over with a champagne-laden heart-shaped tray, decorated with a photograph of Leila and Howard, arms around each other on a beach.

Seconds later they clinked crystal flutes. 'To mutual admiration,' Imogen said.

A silence fell. Not awkward; more thoughtful.

And then... 'Joe?'

'Yes.' His gaze skimmed over her pensive features, over the delicate curve of her neck, the glorious thick dark hair that waterfalled past her shoulders.

'Why didn't you ever mention that you were a surfing champion?'

He stilled. Even knowing that Leila must have mentioned it, he still didn't want to talk about it. 'It's never come up in conversation.'

'It must have been tough to give it up.'

'It was.'

'Like shutting down a fundamental part of yourself?' she asked, quoting his own words back at him.

Dammit. That was what happened when you started to care about other people. It came back to bite you on the bum.

'Yes.'

'Do you regret it?'

'No.'

Clearly the monosyllabic answers weren't doing the trick. Her expression showed a mix of compassion and admiration, and Joe didn't want either.

'I mean it. Holly and Tammy are way, *way* more important to me than being a surfing pro. It was never a question in my mind that there was any choice. And I've never regretted it. Not once. My sisters are two wonderful people, we've built up a cache of incredibly happy memories over the years and we'll continue to do so. I have a career that I love and that I believe has value. Maybe I lost something, but I gained more. Life is what you make it.'

He'd known that all those years before—been determined never to look back and have regrets.

Blue-grey eyes surveyed him and then she stepped forward. Standing on tiptoe, she brushed a feather-light kiss across his cheek before almost leaping backwards.

'I was right. You're a good man.'

Emotions mixed inside him—the desire to pull her into his arms and kiss her properly along with a residue of embarrassment.

'Hey, there were days when it was hard. Don't make me into a saint because I'm not.'

Days when, surrounded by the collapse of the family business, facing the fact that his parents had not been the people he'd believed them to be, trying to help the twins through their grief, all Joe had wanted was his old life back. He had craved the feel of the waves under him, the powerful exhilaration of meeting the challenge of the swell. He'd yearned for the freedom of the sea instead of the net of responsibilities that had sometimes threatened to drown him.

'When did you last surf?' she asked.

'Just after my parents died.'

Her hand rose and one slender finger twirled a tendril of hair. 'I'll do you a deal,' she said.

'What sort of deal?'

'I'll go to that art class tomorrow if you'll go surfing.'

Whoa. 'I'm not sure that's a good idea.'

'Why not?'

'I haven't been on a board in years. I drew a line under it long ago.'

'Then maybe it's time to rub it out. I understand why you gave it up years ago, and I understand how back then you were scared to surf because it would be too painful. But maybe now you could take it up again.'

'I'm too old and too unfit to go back to a professional surfing life, even if I wanted to. Which I don't.'

'Then what's the problem with just surfing because you enjoy it? For you?'

She laid a hand on his arm, her touch heating his skin even through the thick material of his tux.

'It's OK to feel sad that you had to give up something you loved, lived and breathed. It doesn't make your love for the twins any less, and it doesn't make you a bad person if sometimes you resented what fate did to you. Going surfing won't turn you to the dark side.'

How did she *do* that? Understand those deep, dark feelings of guilt and helplessness he'd experienced back then. Discomfort touched him. This was too much, too close, too...*something*. He needed to make a choice. Imogen had offered up a deal: art class in return for a surf session. So he needed to put his man pants on and get on with it.

'OK. Deal. I'll go surfing tomorrow and you'll go to the art class.'

'Deal,' she said.

Joe felt a little light-headed as silence blanketed them once more. This time it was a different silence. The kind that bound them together somehow. His muscles ached with the need to hold her in his arms.

As if on cue, behind them the strains of the music changed from an electro carnival beat to the pure sound of a haunting, melodic song of love and yearning.

The hell with it. He gazed down at her and the words fell from his lips: 'Let's dance.'

It was an awesomely bad idea, but for the life of him he couldn't bring himself to care. No more thinking—right now he wanted to dance with this woman and no other under the starlit sky. Stupid? Probably. But that was the way it was.

Without a word she pushed away from the railings, stood up straight and stepped towards him.

It felt ridiculously right to tug her into his arms, bringing her lush curves flush against him. Biting back a groan, he slid his hand round the slender span of her waist to rest on the flare of her hip.

A shiver ran through her body and she pressed against him, her breasts against his chest, her hair tickling his chin. As lyrics about desire and vows and promises were crooned onto the evening breeze they swayed together, their bodies a perfect fit.

Imogen looped her arms around his neck, her fingers brushing his nape, and this time he couldn't hold back the groan as his pulse-rate rocketed. His hands rested on the curve of her bottom and she looked up at him, lips parted, eyes wide and dark with desire.

How he craved her—with a longing that hollowed his

gut in an intense, deep burn of heat. There was only so much flesh and blood could stand, and his had stood it.

'Let's go,' he said.

Rational thought tried to intervene.

'Unless you want to stay for the photographs? The paps will be here soon.'

'I don't care. Let's go.'

There was no hesitation in her voice—just an acknowledgement that her need was as great as his.

She swallowed. 'Though we should say goodbye to Leila…'

'We'll write a thank-you note.'

Impossible to wait, to make the time to find the bride and groom amongst the crowds. He clasped her hand, interlaced his fingers in hers and pulled her towards the steps leading off the yacht.

Imogen pushed the door of the yurt open, her heart hammering against her ribcage and her whole body one great big mass of need. Following behind her, Joe shoved the door closed and she turned to face him, terrified he'd change his mind even as she knew he wouldn't.

He was no more capable of stopping this—whatever *this* was—than she was.

Every one of her senses felt heightened. Dizziness swirled in her head, and her legs were like blancmange. Staring at Joe, she thought he looked so defined, so focused, against the backdrop of pink canvas. The strength of his jaw, the angle of his cheekbones, the sinful line of his mouth…

Two steps and she was right up close as he leant back against the door and pulled her into his arms. Reaching up, she cupped his jaw, the roughness of his six o'clock shadow tantalising her fingers.

His hand was thrust into her hair and he angled her

face for his kiss before his lips locked over hers in fierce demand. A demand she met without hesitation—met and matched—her entire being consumed by a need only this man, only Joe, could fulfil.

Her greedy fingers tugged at the buttons of his shirt and they pinged to the canvas floor. Not that it mattered. All that mattered was that she could now run her hands over the sculpted muscles of his chest.

He groaned as she stroked his skin, ran a thumb over his nipple. 'I want you, Imo. So bad.'

Joe broke their lip-lock to trail a sizzling stream of kisses along her neck, unerringly finding the sensitive spot that drove her frenzied. She arched her back to give him better access, and then gave a gasp as he scooped her up and resumed their kiss.

He tantalised and tormented her with his tongue as he strode over to the bed and lowered her down, stood above her. The sinful smile that tugged at his lips made her ache with a sudden poignant want as she etched this moment onto her memory. Joe looked younger, carefree, gorgeous, with his brown hair spiked and mussed from her fingers, his eyes dark and dilated with a heat that made her squirm.

As if her movement spurred him on, he shrugged himself out of his shirt, shucked off trousers and boxers.

Her gaze ran over his magnificent body.

'You like?' he asked.

'I want,' she replied and, sitting up, she reached to pull him down onto the bed.

CHAPTER THIRTEEN

IMOGEN ADJUSTED HER sketchpad on the easel, dug her flip-flop-clad toes into the warm crunch of sand and tried to concentrate.

The lecturer was fully living up to his promise—Michael Mallory was brilliant, and in any other circumstances she would be riveted.

Chill out, Imo. So what if Joe hadn't been there when she'd woken up that morning? It was no biggie that he hadn't even left a note. They'd had a deal—she would paint and he would surf. So maybe the waves only worked at a certain time of day…he'd had to rush. Maybe he hadn't been able to find a pen or paper. Maybe he'd written a note and a stray dog had crept into the yurt and eaten it. There were endless possibilities. There was no need for her tummy to be knotted with a sense of dread.

Instead she needed to enjoy the moment and anticipate later. After what they had shared last night—after falling asleep wrapped in each other's arms, her head on his chest, his strong arm encasing her—there was no need for doom and gloom. Later they'd swap stories, have a meal, maybe a glass or two of wine and then…to bed.

And what happens after that, Imo?

Nothing. Nothing happens. Get a grip.

This was lust—pure and simple.

Only…was it more than that? Hadn't they shared things on an emotional level? Could Joe tick the boxes on her list?

'OK,' Michael said. 'Listen up, if you haven't already.'

Imogen jumped and stared at the tall, lanky man who was suddenly standing right in front of her.

He stroked his beard and frowned down at her. 'Yes, that means you. Here is your assignment. You have two hours and then report back here.'

Imogen glanced down at the piece of paper and then around her, realising that the rest of the class had already dispersed.

'Sorry,' she muttered.

'Redeem yourself by producing a worthwhile exercise,' he returned.

Determination seethed inside her. Joe had gone surfing reluctantly, this she knew, and he'd done it so that she could reap the benefits of this class. It was time to do exactly that.

'I will.'

'Good. I've assigned you a place—go there and come back with a land or seascape with a difference. It doesn't have to be technically perfect—draw from your heart and dig deep into your soul.'

Picking up her sketchpad and pencils, she set off. Twenty minutes later she'd reached her destination. It was incredible—a tiny cove of rich golden sand at the foot of a cliff-face that swept the skyline.

As Imogen walked forward her mouth dropped open at the rock formations—arches and shapes that almost defied nature, rock pools galore. Other than herself, the place was completely deserted. It was if she'd gone through a portal and entered another world.

Ah!

That was how she would draw this scene—she would make it slightly alien, use the rock formations to indicate a time portal…subtly distort things… Her brain popped and fizzed with ideas.

Making her way to a handy clump of rocks, she opened her sketchpad and started to draw…

* * *

'Imogen?'

A shadow fell over the sketchbook and she whipped her head up so fast she heard her neck crack.

'Joe.'

'Sorry to interrupt.'

His voice was cool and formal—the tone one you'd use with someone you'd just met and were thoroughly indifferent about. Not someone you'd tangled the sheets with just hours previously.

'That's fine. It's probably good—I'd lost track of time.'

Feeling at a sudden disadvantage, she scrambled to her feet, clutched the sketchbook to her chest. The dreaded leaden feeling returned with a vengeance at the look in his brown eyes—cold with a hint of wariness. She took in his clothes—despite the blaze of the midday sun he wore a crisp white shirt and a lightweight jacket over chinos.

'Didn't pack your Hawaiian shorts?' she asked.

'No.'

'So when are you hitting the waves?'

'That's what I came to tell you.' His voice was even, his features unreadable except for the tension in his jaw. 'I'll have to take a rain check—I have to leave. Now. I've changed my flight but you should stay here—finish the class, soak up some rays.'

'Why do you have to leave?' *Please tell me there's an emergency. Nothing life-threatening but a genuine valid reason for you to go.* 'A work crisis? Do the twins need you?'

'Is that what you want me to say?'

Hell, yeah. Right now Imogen wanted to dig a hole in the sun-scorched sand and bury her head deep, deep down. But she wouldn't do that—that was what she'd done with Steve: refused to see the truth, painted an illusory fictitious relationship world.

'I want you to say the truth.'

'The truth is that after last night I think it's best to cut this interlude short.'

Anger imploded in her: a molten core of volcanic rage. 'Really? That's what you think? Jeez, Joe. What happened to respect? To what you said last night about respecting me? Is this how you show it? Slinking off after sleeping with me? Wham-bam, thank you, ma'am?'

Joe flinched, his mouth set in a grim line.

'That's not how it was. It's not how it is.'

'Then tell me how it is.'

'I don't *know*, goddammit.' He rammed his hands into his pockets and rocked back on his heels. 'I'm not sure what happens after a second one-night stand. It's a situation I've managed to avoid for the past seven years.'

Freaking fabulous. What was she? The flu?

'So this is your answer. Hell, Joe, I'm surprised you even bothered to come out here to tell me you were going. I'd have worked it out soon enough.'

'I didn't want to do that. I don't want us to end badly.'

'Then don't go. Don't run away.'

Joe's guts twisted. Anger at himself pounded his temples. Imogen was hurt; he could see it in the way she hugged that sketchbook to her like some sort of magical shield.

Of course she's hurting, dumb-arse. Your behaviour puts you up for the Schmuck of the Year award.

He should never have let this situation happen. Yet last night he hadn't given Rule Two a thought. Not one. Everything had been obliterated by his need for Imogen—his need to possess her, hold her and savour every centimetre of her. To gaze at the stars and dream.

Madness.

Even looking at her now—so graceful, standing so tall, her eyes challenging—his hands were desperate to break free from his pockets and hold her. The simple sundress she wore exposed her sun-kissed shoulders and the curve of her toned bare arms. So beautiful his heart ached. The sooner he got on that plane the better. And it would be Rule Three all the way. 'No Looking Back'.

'I'm not running away. It's more of a strategic retreat.'

Her lips didn't so much as quiver, and he knew himself the words weren't funny—even if there was an element of truth in them. He knew with a bone-deep certainty that he couldn't spend another night with Imogen.

'I'm leaving because it's best for both of us. Things are getting complicated, and the best way forward now is to draw a line before they complicate further.'

'I thought we were through with drawing lines?'

'Not this one. We got carried away by chemistry again last night; that wasn't meant to happen and I will not risk being driven by lust again.'

Her arms squeezed the sketchbook even tighter as her face leeched of colour and Joe knew she was thinking of her parents' disastrous lust-driven relationship. Which was good—that was what he wanted: for Imogen to be on the same page as he was, in agreement that this had to stop here.

'You want a relationship that isn't based on lust. You want a man who ticks all your boxes and I don't tick any. So it's way better to cut your losses right here and now and go and find him.' His hand fisted in his pockets; the thought of Imogen with another man made him want to hit something—preferably the man. 'It's best for *you*.'

Just like that her shell-shocked face changed, and he knew he'd said the wrong thing as her mouth smacked open in outrage. Eyes narrowed, she stepped forward.

'And what gives you the right to make that decision for me?' Imogen asked. '*I* know what's best for me—not you. All my life people have known what's best for me.

My mother, Steve, and now you. And you've known me all of a few weeks.'

The sarcastic cut of her voice slashed at him and flamed his own emotions to anger. 'You said it yourself, Imogen. That it should only be one night.'

'Then something changed,' she flashed back, before exhaling a sigh. 'Last night *did* happen and I refuse to regret it. Or at least I didn't regret it until now. You know what, Joe? You don't really respect me. Because if you did you would have asked me what I think, how I feel, what I want, what *I* think is best for me. I accept that you need to go, but it's because it's best for *you*. Don't kid yourself or try to kid me you're doing it for me.'

He opened his mouth and then closed it again. Imogen was right. Yet… 'Imogen, I do truly believe this is best for you, but if I'd asked you before I booked that flight what would you have said?'

For a second her gaze dipped away from him, and then she jutted her chin out and met his eyes. 'I'd have suggested we stay here until tomorrow, as planned. I draw, you surf, we have another night. Tomorrow we go home and go our separate ways.'

It sounded so reasonable, so tempting, so….terrifying.

'And what if that slid into one more night? One more week…?'

'Would that be so bad?'

Her voice was small and tight, and Joe hated himself even as he knew what his answer had to be. Everything was sliding out of control, complications abounded, and he needed to get both himself and Imogen out of the line of fire.

'Yes, it would. You're looking for a man who wants a relationship, a white picket fence, a family. I'm not that man. I do *not* tick the boxes.'

'How do you know you couldn't?'

The very thought made his head reel with images of his parents, presenting their perfect married image to the world, supposedly living out their happy-ever-after behind the picket fence. They'd had it all—love, a family, a successful business.

Yet the whole time it had been nothing but a façade.

Joe remembered piecing together the reality of his father's affairs—so many of them with employees and clients. Remembered finding the paperwork showing that his mother was filing for divorce. The family company had been a hotbed of scandal and corruption: funds embezzled, nothing as it was supposed to be, business relationships and personal relationships all a quagmire to be waded through.

The realisation had dawned that everything he'd grown up with had been an illusion. And then it had turned out everything he'd believed he and Leila had was nothing more than another mirage. His whole life had been askew and off-kilter, viewed through the wrong perspective.

He would never put himself in that position again. This thing—whatever it was with Imogen—was meant to fit his rules; Imogen had agreed, goddammit.

'There is no way I can ever tick your boxes. It is not going to happen. Not now, not ever. I do not want complications in my life. You do not want a relationship based on lust.'

'Is that all you think we have?'

'Yes.'

'You really believe that, Joe?'

'I—'

'And do you really believe that having a family and growing old together is just one big complication? Are you really such a coward that you'll always run away from any chance of getting close?'

'Yes, yes and yes again.' Better a coward, than a fool,

enmeshed in an emotional quagmire it would be nigh on impossible to break free from.

Imogen shook her head. 'Then you'd best go. Have a safe flight home.'

'Enjoy the art class.'

It was a monumentally stupid comment, but he was having difficulty unsticking his feet from the sand. Having difficulty doing the thing he needed to do.

'I hope this doesn't make you drop out of it.'

'Don't worry, Joe. Your conscience can rest. I keep my promises. See you around.'

The bitter taste of cowardice and confusion coated his tastebuds as she swivelled and started to walk away from him.

Without so much as a glance back.

He needed to do the same.

It was the only way forward.

CHAPTER FOURTEEN

Three days later

'How are you feeling, hun? Ready to go in there and freeze his balls?'

Imogen managed a smile at Mel's words, truly appreciating her best friend's attempts to cheer her up. Mel had been a rock—had plied her with tea and wine and chocolate and tissues as needed, listened to her rant and pretended not to notice when she cried.

Though who knew why she'd shed a single tear for a man who had made it more than plain that he wanted nothing more to do with her? Humiliation still burned inside her that she hadn't just let him go and feigned indifference. Honestly—she might as well stencil 'Doormat—Use Me' on her forehead.

Yet there had been a moment on that sun-kissed Algarve beach when the grim, haunted expression on Joe's face had twisted her heart—made her want to help with whatever inner demons tormented him.

Hah! More fool her. Inner demons, her foot—Joe had just been terrified that she would go emotional on him. Become a complication to his footloose and fancy-free existence.

Well, she'd show him. Joe had called a meeting at Langley with Peter and Harry, and Peter had asked her to minute it.

Pride straightened her spine. 'I am ready to go in and be arctically professional.'

Mel grinned at her. 'That's my girl. Well, you look the part.'

'Thanks to you! This dress is perfect.'

Imogen smoothed the skirt of the sculpted jersey dress with satisfaction. The demure yet tantalising rounded half-zip neckline, the way the Italian fabric clung to her body, dipped to just above the knee, made her feel professional from the sleek chignon atop her head to her perfectly pedicured pale pink toenails that peeped from a pair of killer heels.

'Show me "The Look".'

Hand on hip, Imogen focused on projecting icy disdain.

'Brilliant!' Mel clapped her hands together. 'Trust me, bits of him will shrivel! Go get 'em, Imo.'

Easier said than done. By the time she'd trekked the tube journey to work the thought of seeing Joe was filling her with a swirl of conflicted emotions. *Come on, Imo.* It was imperative that she crush any lingering stupid hopes, push down the insane lurch of anticipation.

As she approached the boardroom her heart pounded against her ribcage so loudly she'd probably deafen Joe rather than freeze him. Bracing herself, she pushed the boardroom door open and entered. Channelled every bit of her inner ice princess.

The Langley brothers sat on one side of the mahogany table facing Joe, who had his hands flat on the table edge, his gaze directed on Peter.

'You have got to be joking!' Peter Langley leapt to his feet, looking about to vault the table and throttle Joe.

'Peter. Sit down.' Harry half rose and grabbed Peter's arm.

Imogen cleared her throat. 'Sorry I'm late,' she said.

'You aren't.' Harry attempted a smile. 'We started early.

Peter and I just want to know which way the land lies. Come in, Imogen. We'd better minute this.'

'Sure.' Within seconds she'd seated herself at the table, notepad in hand, as foreboding prickled her neck. Something bad was clearly going down.

Yet even her apprehension couldn't prevent her brain from absorbing Joe's appearance. The immaculate charcoal-grey suit with a hint of pinstripe, the bright white shirt, dark blue tie. Professional from the spikes of his hair to the tips of his no doubt shined-up leather shoes. His face was neutral—no trace of any emotion whatsoever. It should be impossible to believe that this man had turned her life upside down, only—*dammit*—it wasn't. Her whole being was on alert, and it was taking every ounce of willpower to keep herself from staring.

'I'm ready,' she said.

Peter waved a hand. 'Go ahead, Joe. Explain your decision.'

'Langley is doing well, but progress has to be sustained and more. Ivan Moreton has come forward with a very lucrative buy-out offer.'

'*Ivan Moreton*?' Disbelief vied with horror.

'Yes.' The syllable gave nothing away. 'The deal he is offering is more than fair. In order to avoid the buy-out Langley needs to meet the criteria set out here over the next two months.' He pushed a bound report across the table. 'Again, I'll go through it for the record.'

As Imogen listened to the points, anger began to simmer. Glancing across at Peter and Harry, she could sense their worry and her tummy twisted in sympathy.

Head back down, she minuted the discussion until the three men had finished. Waited as Joe rose to his feet and shook hands first with Peter and then with Harry.

'You've got my number—any questions, just call. Oth-

erwise I'll be back in two months to review the situation.
I'll see you then.'

Hurt threaded through her building rage—Joe's glance
had barely even skimmed over her, his brown eyes indifferent. Had he really managed to edit her out of his memory banks that easily—just another one-night stand to join
the ranks? Just an anonymous employee in a company he
was grinding in his corporate mill?

Well, hell, she was a lot more than that—and she would
not just stand aside and let him do this. Forget freezing
him—instead her palms itched with the desire to grab him
by the lapels of that tailored suit and shake him until his
teeth rattled. Her hands clenched into fists, all thoughts
of professional cool forgotten

'Excuse me, Joe. Could I have a word before you go?
In private.'

Just great. Exactly what he'd hoped to avoid. The meeting had been bad—for once knowing that his decision was
financially sound and correct was not enough. Nowhere
near enough. As for the effort of keeping his gaze averted
from Imogen—his eyeballs positively ached.

Joe concentrated on maintaining his expression at
strictly neutral. 'Of course.'

The Langley brothers exchanged glances. 'Stay in here,'
Peter suggested. 'Harry and I need to go and come up with
a plan of campaign for the next few months. Imogen, when
you're done here could you please join us in my office?'

'Sure.'

She rose to her feet as they left the boardroom, and Joe
braced himself to withstand the sheer force of her beauty
and her anger.

'What can I do for you, Imogen?' he asked, sitting back
at the table.

She slammed her palms down on the mahogany table-top. 'You can explain what the hell *that* was all about.'

'Meaning…?'

'Meaning I thought you said that you didn't like to close companies down.'

'I don't—and if you read the minutes you just took you'll see that I didn't.'

'Huh. Those criteria are nigh on impossible.'

'No, they aren't. They are difficult, I grant you, but they are doable.'

'Provided Harry doesn't have another heart attack and Peter doesn't relapse into another breakdown from the stress.'

Her voice caught and, heaven help him, guilt shoved him hard in the chest.

'How could you do this, Joe? It's wrong.'

'I have no choice—Ivan Moreton's offer is very generous.'

'Of course it is. That's because there is nothing Ivan wants more than to take this company down. He loathes Peter and Harry. You must realise that?'

Joe rubbed a hand over his face. 'Yes, I do. But that dislike gives Langley a profitable way out. He's even promised to keep the majority of staff.'

'So he can rub their noses in his triumph. Plus, he knows damn well neither Peter nor Harry would ever work for him.'

Something tugged in his chest; face flushed, eyes sparking, Imogen looked so beautiful he wanted to help. Wanted to give her whatever she wanted. Which was exactly why it was time to close this interview down. Before he did something stupid. *Again*.

Rising to his feet, he shook his head. 'This meeting is over, Imogen. I've given Langley a chance.'

For a second a doubt assailed him. *Had* his decision

been strictly business? Somewhere deep down had he rea-
soned that even if he'd refused to give Imogen a chance he
could at least offer the company she loved one?

'I suggest you go out there and take it.'

A small frown creased her brow as her blue-grey eyes
surveyed him.

He held out a hand. 'Goodbye, Imogen. And good luck.'

Her fingers lay in his for one brief final moment. 'Goodbye, Joe.'

Two months later

Imogen drew in a deep breath and looked around her tiny
new studio apartment with approval. Spick and span, with
nothing that even the most exacting parent could complain
about. Fresh flowers on the small foldaway table, which
was open and beautifully laid, complete with ice bucket for
the champagne currently in the fridge. Hell, this would be a
celebration even if it killed her. If it wasn't, and her parents
went loopy, then she'd just drink the damn bottle herself.

Heaven knew she deserved it after the past months—
but it had been worth every single lost moment of sleep as
she and all of the Langley team had pulled together and
managed to meet every criterion on Joe's list. Now Peter
and Harry had met with Joe and Langley was safe—the
knowledge was a constant warm glow inside her.

But that wasn't the reason for this lunch. Apprehension
fizzed in her veins and as if on cue the doorbell rang. Her
heart beating a nervous rhythm against her ribcage, she
crossed the floor and pulled the door open.

'Hey, Mum. Hey, Dad.'

Panic roiled in her tummy at the sheer enormity of what
she'd done and what she had to tell them. Even so, the certainty that she was right calmed her—Joe had been correct. She couldn't live her life for her parents, no matter

how much she loved them. Any more than he would expect his sisters to follow a path of *his* choosing just because he had chosen to take responsibility for them.

Instead he'd encouraged them to live their dreams, and he spoke of them with love—never disappointment. Eva hadn't ever been able to do the same, and whilst that was perhaps wrong, what had also been wrong was Imogen's compliance in that. That was why Joe had urged her to embrace art.

Joe. Why did anything and everything always come back to Joe?

'Imogen? What's the matter? We haven't come all this way just to watch you daydream.'

Eva Lorrimer's querulous voice pulled her into the present.

'Sorry, Mum.' Imogen hauled in breath—no point dressing this up. 'Thank you for coming. I've got some fantastic news. I've been accepted into art college.'

Silence plummeted as Eva opened and closed her mouth, whilst Jonathan Lorrimer shifted from foot to foot.

'Is this some sort of joke?' Her mother had gone pale, her forehead pinched.

'No, Mum. It's for real. It's a top London college and I can start in January.' Imogen tried for a laugh…winced at the strangled gargle she achieved. 'So you know what to get me for Christmas.'

Eva shook her head. 'How could you be so stupid, Imogen? After everything I went through for you…'

Guilt surfaced, along with a hefty dose of self-doubt, but then she pushed her shoulders back and adhered her feet to the carpet. Joe might not be in her life, but he had taught her something life-changing. That life was for living and it was *her* life to live.

'Mum!'

To her surprise the interruption worked and Eva stopped talking.

'I know I've never managed to achieve what you wanted me to achieve, but that doesn't mean I'm stupid. Just because maths and science aren't my thing it doesn't make me useless.' She could feel a weight lift from her shoulders, was liberated by the words.

'I... I...' Eva rallied. 'I never thought that—I just wanted what was best for you. I wanted you to make something of yourself.'

'And I have done that. I'm proud of my work at Langley.'

'Being a PA is a good steady job...'

'It is—and I'm a good PA. But I've been more than that at Langley and now I want to pursue my dream, Mum. Not yours, but mine.'

'And end up penniless, knocking on my door for help?'

'No! I've thought all this through. Langley is safe now, and I've arranged with Peter to keep working there part-time. I've got a manageable student loan. I'll show you the figures, if you like. I can make this work *and* pay my own way. I'm so excited—please be excited for me.'

'I'm excited for you.'

Swivelling on her trainer-clad foot, Imogen surveyed her father with surprise.

'Truly I am, Imo. I may not have made it yet, but if you've been accepted into art college then maybe I can live vicariously through you. Well done, poppet.'

Poppet. He hadn't called her that for so many years. Not since those rare times when he'd sat with her as a child and shown her how to draw. Until either Eva had put a stop to it or he'd disappeared back to his studio, leaving her to fend for herself. But at least now he could find it in himself to be happy for her, rather than begrudge her a success he hadn't had, and she was grateful for that.

'Thanks, Dad.'

'*Tchah!* Well, *I'm* not excited for you, Imogen.' Eva sniffed. 'I can't stop you, and I won't try, but I still think you're making a grave mistake. You'll get caught up in this art malarkey and the rest of your life will pass you by. When will you have time to meet a nice man to settle down with?'

The question hurt, and she blinked hard as an image of Joe shot into her head. *Nice. Settle down.* Not words she associated with Joe—but it didn't matter. Like it or not, he'd insinuated himself into her heart and it was proving hard to prise him out. But she would—even if she had to get a chisel.

'You lost Steve, and now—'

'Steve loves Simone. And next week we can all dance at their wedding and wish them well.'

And she meant it—the thought of attending no longer had the sting it had held before. Steve and Simone were happy—that much was clear from the one conversation she'd had with Steve after he had voluntarily reimbursed her for the cost of the cruise. Further evidence had been provided by the stream of happy photos that Simone flooded social media with on a daily basis.

True, her stomach still dipped at the idea of being pointed out as the poor little ex, but she'd manage. At least she would be able to foil the sympathetic stares and prurient curiosity with her college news.

'So,' she said firmly. 'How about we open the champagne?'

One day later

Exhilaration shot through Joe's veins at the familiar feel of the surfboard under his feet. He felt weightless, suspended in time and nature, at one with the elements.

The power of the sea was both awe-inspiring and thrilling. Sheer adrenalin pumped in his blood as he caught the wave, and the screech of a seagull blended with the pounding in his ears, the tang of the sea spray on his skin causing sheer joy.

Just like the way he felt when he was with Imogen.

One week later

OK. She could do this. Imogen gazed out of the window as the train pulled in to the old-fashioned Devon station and she tried to block out her parents' bickering voices.

'Don't see why any of us are coming to this damned wedding at all,' Jonathan muttered. 'Though I suppose if you feel you need to go, Imo, the least we can do is come to give you some moral support.'

Eva sighed. 'I've explained time and again that we are going to this wedding because Steve was once part of our lives and he is the son of one of my oldest acquaintances.'

'The same acquaintance who looks at me as though I'm something she stepped in,' Jonathan grumbled as he lugged a suitcase onto the platform.

'Guys…'

Some things would never change—she would probably be playing peacemaker between her parents for ever. Yet it could be worse; she might have lost her parents in a tragedy like Joe had…

Not again. No thoughts of Joe, today of all days.

Raising her voice to drown out her thoughts, Imogen waved placating hands at her parents. 'For whatever reasons we are all here now, so let's just get on with it. At least the scenery is gorgeous, the church is beautiful, and maybe we can find time for a proper cream tea.'

A taxi ride later and Imogen scanned the churchyard, bracing herself for the sight of friends and acquaintances all waiting to pounce.

Instead…

She blinked and dropped her knuckles from her eyes
in the nick of time. Rubbing her eyes was not an option—
not with the amount of make-up she had on. It must be
a hallucination, but however many times she blinked the
man remained there.

Solid and real—he looked just like Joe.

Hallucinating—that was what she was doing.

The hallucination headed purposefully towards them,
dressed to kill in the same dark grey suit he'd worn to
Leila's wedding. Her nerves skittered, her tummy somer-
saulted—maybe it really was Joe.

'Hello, Imogen.'

'Joe. Um…what are you doing here?'

He raised his eyebrows. 'I'm here for the wedding, of
course.'

Gathering her wits together, she managed an introduc-
tion, saw her mother's eyes scan from her face to Joe's
and braced herself again. But to her surprise Eva tugged
on her husband's arm.

'Come on, Jonathan. Let's get inside. Imo and her friend
can follow us. I want a chance to talk to Clarissa.'

Her brain fried, scrambled and poached all at the same
time—and if that wasn't bad enough all she wanted to do
was launch herself at his chest and hold on for dear life.

Once her parents were out of earshot Imogen forced her
vocal cords to obey her brain's command. 'So you're real?'

His eyebrows rose as his lips quirked upward. 'Last
time I checked.'

Her whole being drank him in. She noticed that his hair
was longer…even spikier. There was a touch of strain about
his eyes, and as he rubbed his neck in that oh, so familiar
gesture she would have sworn he was nervous.

'Is everything OK?'

'It is now. You're looking good.'

'Thank you. You too.' Hauling in breath, she asked the million-dollar question. 'Why are you here? Really?'

'I'm keeping my part of the bargain. You come to Leila's wedding, I come to Steve's—remember?'

Imogen hauled her senses into line. 'I kind of assumed all deals were off due to unexpected complications.'

'Nope.' His gaze latched on to hers with a seriousness that made her tingle all over. 'I've been surfing. All deals are back on.'

He'd gone surfing. Imogen's heart skipped in the sure knowledge that he'd done that out of honour. But that didn't change anything.

'I'm glad,' she said simply. 'And I appreciate this, but I'll be fine on my own.'

'OK.'

A curl of disappointment rippled inside her.

'I'll see you in there, then,' he continued.

'Huh?'

'I scored myself an invite of my own.'

'How?'

'I gate-crashed the wedding rehearsal and threw myself on Simone's mercy. I think she was quite pleased to see me.'

'You did what? What did you tell them?'

'I told them the truth. That I needed to see you. We need to talk. A bit more privately. There's a bench round the corner. We've got a bit of time before the ceremony.'

Imogen hesitated.

'Please.'

The word disarmed her. Joe was used to giving orders—plus he'd come all this way—plus... Plus she wanted to be with him, wanted to make the most of every minute, and wouldn't a proper closure be better than the way it had ended? No doubt that was why he was here.

'OK. But we can't be long.'

She followed him through the picturesque graveyard, tried to concentrate on the old gravestones, the feeling of history and peace, the autumnal smell in the air, the red-brown leaves on the trees.

'Here we go. It's secluded enough here and out of the wind. I checked.'

'How forward-thinking of you,' Imogen managed as she attempted to try and think through a haze of misplaced happiness. It was as though there had been a bit of her missing and now she was whole. She needed to get a grip.

'Isn't it?'

His eyes raked over her as she sat down and spread the swirl of her turquoise dress out so that he couldn't get too close. Close would be a bad idea. The man was uptight, rule-orientated, cold. A man who thought three nights was a commitment he couldn't deal with. But despite herself she craved the warmth of his body.

Her memory was flooded with the way he'd held her, the way he'd shown her so much about herself, the way he'd made love to her.

'Joe, it's OK. I'm OK. You don't have to explain anything. Everything has worked out fine. As you know, better than anyone, Langley is safe. I'm not going to melt down or be permanently affected by the time we had together or the way you behaved. Though, for the record, it sucked.'

'You're right. It did. And I'm sorry.'

The flare of hope she hadn't even realised she'd harboured died. He was here to apologise—nothing more.

'Apology accepted. Now, please don't feel you have to stay. Steve and I are good. We've worked out our differences. I can more than manage on my own.'

The words were true but oh, how she wished it wasn't like this. Her heart ached; her chest was banded with pain.

'So I guess this is goodbye. Again.'

* * *

This was *so* not the way it was supposed to play out—hard to understand how he who could grasp control of any boardroom meeting—anywhere, any time—couldn't manage this situation.

Panic sheened the nape of his neck with moisture. Imogen was saying goodbye—he'd obviously blown any available bridge sky-high.

'No.'

Was that croak his voice? Time to step up—because no way was he losing this woman without at least a fight.

'No,' he repeated firmly. 'It's not.'

'There is nothing more to say.'

'That's where you are so very wrong. There is a load more to say. But first I need to say the most important thing.'

'What's that?'

'I love you.'

Joe wasn't sure what he'd expected, but the sceptical rise of her eyebrows wasn't it—nor the determined shake of her head as she slipped her hands under her thighs.

'Don't, Joe…'

'Don't what?'

'Lie.'

'Lie?' She thought he was *lying*?

'It doesn't make sense. I haven't seen hide nor hair of you for two months. Last time I saw you, you couldn't even contemplate more than two nights with me—this is taking "absence makes the heart grow fonder" too far.'

He was making an incredible mess of this. Had he really thought she'd fall into his arms in a swoon of delight? He needed to make her believe him. This was his last chance.

'Imogen, I love you. I loved you back then and I love you now. That's a fact. Love isn't logical, and you can't put it in a tick-box. I panicked on that beach on the Algarve because for seven years I'd lived by my self-imposed rules and then you came into my life and changed everything. Broke down all the barriers I'd built to keep my life from complications.'

Imogen swept her fringe to one side as she contemplated his words. 'I'm not sure I want to feature in your life as an unwanted complication.'

'You won't.' He shoved a hand through his hair and tried to summon up coherence. 'I…I've done a lot of thinking over these past two months. And I've realised what I did after my parents died. I closed down.'

'That's understandable. It's part of the grieving process.'

'It was more than that. They left a mess behind them. Turned out their marriage was on the rocks and the family business was so far up the proverbial creek a hundred paddles wouldn't have been enough.'

He shrugged.

'I had no idea. I thought they had an idyllic marriage and the business was thriving. It was all an illusion. Tax evasion, fraud, infidelity, wrongdoing… My father was higher than a kite, funded by clients' money. Women… clients, colleagues, secretaries…he slept with them all. My mother turned a blind eye for the money, but the money was running out so she was filing for divorce. It was all very…complicated.'

'Oh, Joe.'

Her face was scrunched up in compassion as she twisted her body to face him, placed her hand on his thigh, her touch so warm, so right.

'I can't begin to imagine how confusing, how incredibly emotional it must have been for you. To have all your memories twisted—and you couldn't even ask them why. No wonder you decided the best way forward was no complications.'

He shifted his body to face her, amazed at how easy, how right it felt to share.

'All I wanted was to sort it all out, look after the twins and make sure I never let complication into my life again. So that's what I did. Then I met you and you changed everything; you've shown me how to feel again, to care, to love, and I don't care how complicated it is. I'll become the man you want me to be, Imogen, if I have to try all my life long. Give me that tick-list and I'll do my best.'

'No!'

The word hurt, slammed into him like a cannonball. But then she shifted along the bench, her warmth right next to him.

'There is no tick-list,' she said. 'I've shredded it and burnt the scraps.'

'Why?'

'Because you made me see what a stupid idea it was. How can someone conform to a tick-list? I tried to do that. For Steve. I tried to make myself fit his list and the result was a nightmare.' She laid her small hand on his thigh. 'I can *so* see why you closed down after your parents died. I didn't close down, but I built myself a comfort zone and I was too scared to leave it—too scared I'd repeat my parents' mistakes, too scared I'd be like my father and fail. Meeting you changed that, made me see how exhilarating it is to push the boundaries and go for what you want.'

She smiled at him—a smile that lit up his world.

'I've been accepted at art school.'

Happiness for Imogen and the world opening out to her warmed his chest. 'That's amazing news, sweetheart.'

'It all started from that art class. Mike, the lecturer, made me promise to keep in touch and he really encouraged me. He's been so supportive and...'

Jealousy and pain tackled him at the same time, twisted

his gut with a hurt he knew he had to conceal. 'So…you and this Mike guy…?'

'No! Don't be daft.'

Blue-grey eyes widened as she stared at him.

'Oh, Joe. Don't you get it? I love you.'

'You do?'

'Yes, I do. Every bit of you—from the spikes in your hair to the tips of your toes. I love how you've made me strive to live the dream, the way you make me feel protected and like I can do anything. I love how you talk about your sisters and I love how you give one hundred per cent of yourself to what you do. I just *love* you. Full-stop.'

He grinned at her, his heart full with the sheer joy of hearing the words. 'One thing you should know, though…'

'What's that?'

'I'm expecting plenty of lustful goings-on in our marriage, whatever you think.'

In one fluid movement she landed on his lap and cupped his face in her hands. 'Well, Mr McIntyre, that's lucky—because I wouldn't have it any other way.' Then she froze. 'Did you say marriage? You mean…?'

'If you'll have me. Imogen, I can't imagine anything better than being your husband and waking up every morning with you in my arms. I want it all—white picket fence, kids, the lot.' He pulled her closer, his arms round the slender span of her waist. 'Because what we have, Imogen, is way more than lust. We have liking and respect and love.'

She nodded. 'I know. That's why these past two months I've missed you so damn much. Talking to you…laughing with you. I've missed the way you need that first cup of coffee, the way your hair spikes up. I've missed your scowl and your smile. Your touch, your taste, your smell.'

'I know exactly what you mean, sweetheart. I've spent weeks trying to stick to Rule Three and not look back. But you—you've haunted my days and my nights. I'd wake up in the night and swear I could feel your hair tickling my chin. So many memories… I couldn't stop looking back, though God knows I tried. Filling my days with work and…'

'Your nights?'

'My nights were filled with fantasies of you. I love you, Imogen Lorrimer. You've made me see love can be real. Not an illusion. So, Imogen, if you want me in your life I oh, so definitely want you in mine. For ever. Will you marry me?'

'Absolutely, Joe. I am all yours. For ever.'

He smiled a smile that lit her world—a smile that made her feel like the most beautiful, wonderful, desirable woman in the world. A smile that spoke volumes, spoke of everlasting love and all-encompassing joy.

'Then let's live the dream, Imogen. Starting now.'

EPILOGUE

Dear Diary
In case you've forgotten me, as I've neglected you
shamefully over the past few months, my name is
Imogen Lorrimer—until tomorrow, when I will be-
come Imogen McIntyre. Because tomorrow I am
marrying Joe McIntyre, who I no longer have to
dream is in my bed because he has taken to making
a regular appearance there. Naked.

I love him.

Think sexy rumpled hair. That I love to run my
fingers through. Think chocolate—the expensive
kind—brown eyes that gaze at me with love in their
depths. Oh, and a body that I plan to worship for
the rest of my life.

Joe is kind and loving and altogether perfect. He
has taken up surfing again and, believe me, watch-
ing Joe on a surfboard is a privilege. He's thinking
of setting up some sort of surf school for teenagers
in the future. Our long-term plan is to move out of
London and settle in Cornwall—though first I want
to finish college.

Which is utterly amazing—and Langley has been
fantastic at being flexible so I can work and attend
college. Mum is way happier about the whole art col-
lege scenario now I am marrying Joe. In fact I don't
know how he's done it but he's even charmed her into

admitting one of my pictures was 'not bad'. Which from Mum is a compliment of the highest order.

Dad has found work in an art supply shop, and whilst he still spends all his spare time in his studio, I have the feeling Mum and Dad are getting on a little bit better.

Holly and Tammy are fantastic—it's like having the siblings I always dreamed of. They are going to be bridesmaids, with Mel as chief bridesmaid. So, you see, life could not be better.

Tomorrow, dear diary, I will be walking down the aisle towards Joe, and I know with all my heart and soul that this is the man I will love for the rest of my life. And that he will love me right back.

For ever
Night-night
Imogen xxx

* * * * *

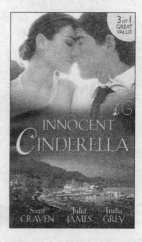

4_ST_5